PICKERING PUBLIC LIBRARY

3 3081 0011 W9-BVA-643

ELIZABETH TAYLOR

(1912–1975) was born Elizabeth Coles in Reading, Berkshire. The daughter of an insurance inspector, she was educated at the Abbey School, Reading, and after leaving school worked as a governess and, later, in a library. At the age of twenty-four she married John William Kendall Taylor, a businessman, with whom she had a son and a daughter. She lived much of her married life in the village of Penn in Buckinghamshire.

Elizabeth Taylor wrote her first novel, *At Mrs Lippincote's* (1945), during the war while her husband was in the Royal Air Force. This was followed by *Palladian* (1946), *A View of the Harbour* (1947), *A Wreath of Roses* (1949), *A Game of Hide-and-Seek* (1951), *The Sleeping Beauty* (1953), *Angel* (1957), *In a Summer Season* (1961), *The Soul of Kindness* (1964), *The Wedding Group* (1968), *Mrs Palfrey at the Claremont* (1971) and *Blaming*, published posthumously in 1976. She has also published four volumes of short stories: *Hester Lilly and Other Stories* (1954), *The Blush and Other Stories* (1958), *A Dedicated Man and Other Stories* (1965) and *The Devastating Boys* (1972). Elizabeth Taylor has written a book for children, *Mossy Trotter* (1967); her short stories have been published in the *New Yorker*, *Harper's Bazaar*, *Harper's* magazine, *Vogue* and the *Saturday Evening Post*, and she is included in *Penguin Modern Stories 6*.

Critically Elizabeth Taylor is one of the most acclaimed British novelists of this century, and in 1984 *Angel* was selected as one of the Book Marketing Council's "Best Novels of Our Time". Virago publishes twelve of her sixteen works of fiction.

VIRAGO
MODERN
CLASSIC

NUMBER
278

ELIZABETH TAYLOR

At Mrs Lippincote's

WITH AN AUTOBIOGRAPHICAL SKETCH
BY THE AUTHOR

PICKERING PUBLIC LIBRARY
CENTRAL BRANCH

Virago

Published by VIRAGO PRESS Limited 1988
41 William IV Street, London WC2N 4DB

First published in Great Britain by Peter Davies 1945

Copyright © Elizabeth Taylor 1945

Elizabeth Taylor article Copyright © N.Y.T.N.S. 1953

All rights reserved

British Cataloguing in Publication Data
Taylor, Elizabeth, *1912–1975*
 At Mrs Lippincote's. — (Virago
 modern classics).
 I. Title
 823′.914 [F] PR6039.A928

 ISBN 0-86068-538-1

Printed in Great Britain by Cox & Wyman
of Reading, Berks.

Elizabeth Taylor

I was born in 1912 in Reading, Berkshire, and went to school there at the Abbey School, where I handed in essays with as much trepidation as I now feel before reading reviews of my books. When I left school, we moved to the country in Buckinghamshire—to a village where I had spent many happy holidays as a child. I drifted into being a governess and went on writing novels in the evenings as I had done for years. (None published until after I was thirty.) I liked teaching children, but those who have a lifetime of it have my admiration, too. Children's conversations are lively and often poetic, their truthfulness exhilarating, not shocking. I enjoy writing about them, but especially if they are set against a background of adults.

I was married in 1936 and we live now in the village of Penn in Buckinghamshire. We have two children—a son, Renny, who is sixteen, and a daughter, Joanna, who is twelve. I am always disconcerted when I am asked for my life story, for nothing sensational, thank heavens, has ever happened. I dislike much travel or change of environment, and prefer the days (each with its own domestic flavor) to come round almost the same, week after week. Only in such circumstances can I find time or peace in which to write. I also very much like reading books in which practically nothing ever happens.

Domestic jobs I find pleasant except for the guilty feeling that I ought to be working—that is, writing. Only cooking seems important enough to stave off that feeling, and cooking and shopping are true pleasures. Going off in a country bus with large shopping baskets is always an adventure.

But in the end, one must return to one's own work. Writing, which was easy to me only when I was a child, becomes more and more a difficult thing which I cannot escape. Unlike other jobs, it goes along with me everywhere—even on holiday. A writer cannot rest from continually observing and being assailed by impressions. His imagination is too easily touched off. Holidays are, in fact, an especial encouragement to work because of the anonymity of one's surroundings—the endearing impersonality of hotel bedrooms. At home, my desk overlooks the garden. For that reason I never use it, except to stuff it with letters which, especially the children's from school, I can never throw away. I usually write sitting on the floor by the fire—in pencil in school exercise books. As I rewrite a great deal, so that sometimes a sentence in its evolution takes a whole page of scratching out, I copy the penciled version in pen into the beautiful stiff-boarded marbled books I coveted as a child. This is a peaceful occupation—the only part of writing which is not a despairing struggle. Then, when I am alone in the house I read it all aloud. This often reveals repetitions I had not observed, or monotony in the construction of sentences, or improbabilities of dialogue.

When, at the end of the war, I first had a novel published, I received the proofs in trembling excitement. Now I am filled with anxiety, for I am a poor proof-reader.

As for reviews, I do not know how some writers manage not to read them. Curiosity always leads me into the trap. Good reviews seem to be extraordinary kindnesses, and although one is encouraged and uplifted by them they never seem to ring true as do the bad ones.

The reading I do is often re-reading. Jane Austen is very re-readable; there are always unremembered delights. I sometimes read "Tristram Shandy" backwards, thinking that two can play that game of kicking the insides out of the clock. Then I like Tchehov, Turgenev, Aksorkov, the Brontës (not leaving out Anne who writes so tenderly of

vi

the English scene), Hardy, Henry James, James Joyce, Virginia Woolf. Of present-day writers my favourites are I. Compton-Burnett (one of the greatest writers in our history), Elizabeth Bowen, Colette, Eudora Welty. I am sure there are many men whose books I have enjoyed, but their names do not seem to come readily to mind. I do not read much poetry, or rather, do not break much new ground in it. Of poets now living I know very little, except T.S. Eliot, whom I re-read often, especially the "Four Quartets", which I find haunting, resonant and moving.

I think I have no hobbies. In my spare time I like to look at pictures, to write letters to my friends, or just to reflect upon the English climate—a subject which is endlessly fascinating and elusive, of which one is rarely unconscious. I do not know where English literature—or the lovely English landscape—would be without this weather.

This article by Elizabeth Taylor first appeared in the *New York Herald Tribune*, Book Review (Section 6), October 11th, 1953.

At Mrs Lippincote's

CHAPTER 1

"DID THE OLD MAN die here? What do you think?" Julia asked, as her husband began to come upstairs.

"Old man? What old man?"

She stood on the shadowy landing with its six white doors.

"What old man?" asked Roddy once more, coming up and putting his arm along her shoulders.

"The husband. Mr Lippincote. Oh, how I wish we needn't live in other people's houses!"

"What if he did?"

Yes, what indeed? The dead cannot communicate with the living, or do harm to them. Julia believed that: there are, of course, those who do not. She knew his death could make no difference to her, even if it had happened in that room, upon that bed. Heart trouble (angina pectoris, which people die from so often in novels) had been the end of him, not some loathsome disease. The heart gave its last tick, the blood having slowed, the limbs stiffened. Bodies are hastened away before further changes occur. 'A place for everything,' she thought, and giggled. But, nevertheless, hung back till Roddy had preceded her into the bedroom.

"Anyhow," he said, seeing her poor face, "people mostly die in nursing homes these days." That was Roddy all over—that leader of men, who did not know how the world lived, discounting all those who do not go to nursing homes, and Mrs Lippincote herself who believed in dying, if possible, upon the bed where one was born, and who had herself closed (without horror, only grief) the eyes of her dead husband in this very room a month or two before.

The room itself was filled with mahogany—wardrobe, chest, tall-boy, medicine cupboard—with a bluish sheen on

5

it this damp evening. The window was in one corner and was semi-circular, for it formed, as one saw from the outside, a little turret with a gilt weather-vane upon it. Green leaves —of some not very interesting tree, perhaps a sycamore— pressed up close to the panes. But there was every comfort Julia switched on the electric fire and changed the room completely; the mahogany shone with pink now, and the trees outside were at once discounted.

There were all the trunks, one with the lid off and frothing chaotically with her underclothes, for she had dived to the bottom in search of handkerchiefs. Oh, God! Of course, they were not there. She found, however, some talcum powder and a packet of envelopes which she needed.

As for a handkerchief . . . sniffing miserably, she had begun to rummage in the pockets of Roddy's greatcoat. She did this aloofly, for husbands' pockets, since they were the subject of music-hall jokes, were always to be scorned and avoided. He did not, apparently, carry handkerchiefs. "Now, what are you up to?" he had asked, coming into the bedroom with yet another case. "My dear Julia, this trunk! You dive like a mole and leave disorder in your train."

He considered a list in his hand. "Handkerchiefs, stock-ings, small blue suitcase," he read out.

There was the blue suitcase on the chest, and here were the keys in his pocket. He clicked open the catches and handed her a nice white handkerchief. What could have been simpler?

But she had already, in desperation, blown her nose upon a piece of tissue-paper from her hat-box. Now, she sat by the fire and considered this incident. Roddy and Eleanor, who unpacked alone in the next room, were alike in this: they never dived frantically but considered lists which they had drawn up before. 'They have patience and method,'

6

she decided, ' but they are always too late. I, with my make-shift, have always arrived before them.'

" There are some things you cannot acquire," she told Roddy. " These lists, for instance. They are not in me. It is a flair. Like making pastry. You are either born with a cool quick hand or you are not. It can never be taught."

Such reflections were always thrown away upon Roddy. " I have never complained about your pastry," he assured her and then, remembering some book or other, written by a woman, on *Happy Marriages, How to Make, Maintain, and Endure Them*, he basely and unnecessarily betrayed his own mother. " Her pastry is always heavier than yours," he concluded.

' Those tarts! ' she thought. The greyish slabs embedded with mauve cherries. But he shouldn't have said it. ' I wouldn't like Oliver to, one day.' Her legs, scorching before the fire, resembled blood-red mottled marble.

" I can't do any more! " she said. " Do let's leave it. Can't we unpack the rest to-morrow? "

" I'm on duty to-morrow night, and I must unpack my own."

" Oh, well then! " She pulled on some grubby quilted slippers. " I'll go and get the supper."

She peeped round the door of Oliver's room as she crossed the landing. He lay as still as a rock, yet as soon as she withdrew, sprang up in bed and called her. She went back only too gladly, bent to kiss him, laying her cheek against his own smooth thin one, breathing the warm cleanness of him. His arms twisted like snakes about her neck.

" I've forgotten what the outside of the house is like. Except the tower. I never went into a tower before." He was busily, under cover of the conversation, collecting hair-pins from the top of her head. Down came her hair, flopping heavily, frond after frond, against his face. He laughed but

7

still held on. "When you get inside the tower, though, it is just like an ordinary room." She could feel his heart racing beneath his ribs.

"Darling, I must go. I want my supper."

"Yes, so do I want mine."

"Hush! I shouldn't have come in. You're being stupid and naughty."

"Why shouldn't I have supper? I am *growing*," he cried, loosening his hold of her in his anger. "I need food."

When she got to the door, "Good-night, devil!" he called cheerfully.

"What was that I heard you call your mother?" Roddy stood gravely in the doorway.

"Shush!" Julia laid a hand on his sleeve and drew him back on to the landing. When Roddy said 'Your mother' in that way, she felt ridiculous.

"I won't have so much rudeness," he said loudly as she shut the door.

"Only fun," she whispered. "Let him go to sleep."

"You woke him up."

She went downstairs, groping through shadow, not knowing where the light switches were, her hands passing over the walls, which felt clammy and unfamiliar. The house had a closed smell. A little light came through some blood-red glass at the front door. Through an archway hung with plush, she came to the kitchen. It was like the baser side of someone's nature. Beyond the plush curtains, the house put aside all show of decency. Here, there was no doubt about the suggestion of damp. Beads of moisture lay upon the walls. She rattled curtains across the window and put on the light.

This room, she supposed, represented what was fitting and decent for the working class. On this side of the arch, varnished deal was preferred, wallpaper of brown and pink

8

flowers, a brown tablecloth reaching to the floor and a plant with thick grey velvety leaves. Then down a hollowed stone step into a brick scullery where a refrigerator whirred and water dropped bleakly and with regularity into a bowl. She opened a cupboard and was frightened by a soup tureen the size of a baby's bath. In another cupboard a dozen meat dishes of very slightly varying sizes, white with a wreath of inky flowers, the glaze traced with faint sepia cracks.

'That is how Mrs Lippincote set up house,' she told herself.

The gas-stove was rusty, but she unhooked a great iron frying-pan, wiped it out, stabbed at some sausages with a fork and laid them in a row in the pan. The ghosts of servants seemed to hover in the place—Mrs Beeton servants, with high caps and flying bows to their aprons. But the ghosts haunted; they did not help or encourage.

She went listlessly into the dining-room, up and down steps and through the arch into the other world: carpets, instead of linoleum; mahogany, not deal.

Roddy's cousin, Eleanor, had come down, had drawn the curtains and put on the gas-fire. The room looked bright and pleasant in its old-fashioned way.

Eleanor, with a newspaper spread on a chair, had climbed up to examine a wedding group.

"Oh, Julia! These clothes. The tucks and the scrolls of braid and all the little buttons on the bosoms!"

"And the bosoms themselves," said Julia. "Let me!" she begged. She took her place on the chair and gazed at the yellowing photograph. "Mrs Lippincote!" she murmured. "That's the old man, then! He looks as if he were made of wax."

Indeed, he looked full of apologies as if at the thought of the indiscretions lying ahead of him; but his bride, hand-

9

ling her bouquet masterfully, had already, it appeared, begun her business of smilingly controlling him.

" I never like seeing a bride so large," said Eleanor with a titter.

Julia gazed as if lost. There they stood, young, surrounded by prosperous-looking parents, all pleased, sure and comfortable. Yet did not one set of parents look milder, on a smaller scale than the other? Had she, in fact, married a little beneath her?

" Girls all had the same shaped faces in those days,' Eleanor was saying. " Rounded, rather thick in the jaw, a low of eyebrow and a fuzz of hair."

Yes, all the bridesmaids were alike, but were perhaps sisters. A strip of patterned carpet and some pots of fern had been arranged outside a conservatory. The sun had shone. Two young men lay, leaning each on an elbow, at the feet of the others. With their ankles crossed, they looked like two splendid fishes lying there.

' And now it's all finished,' Julia thought. 'They had that lovely day and the soup tureen and meat dishes, servants with frills and streamers, children. They set out that day as if they were laying the foundations of something. But it was only something which perished very quickly, the children scattered, the tureen draped with cobwebs, and now the widow, the bride, perhaps at this moment unfolding her napkin alone at a table in a small private hotel down the road.'

The smell of burning sausages could not reach beyond the archway. Julia remembered and leapt from the chair Eleanor dealt out odd forks and some knives like scimitars over the tablecloth.

" This is what they call a ' cruet '," she told Roddy, who came in rubbing his soap-smelling hands. He smiled at her.

Julia came in with the pound of burnt sausages lying on the smallest dish.

"You can't expect mustard on the first night," she warned Roddy, who thought what a very few seconds it would have taken to mix. Two and a half sausages for her and Eleanor, three for Roddy. There was bread and cheese as well, and some egg sandwiches left over from the train.

"I could wish for a drink," said Julia, passing her hand over her face in great weariness.

"I can't take you into the Ante-room to-night," said Roddy in a satisfied way. "It isn't ladies' night."

"Can't we have a drink in this damned place, without relying on the caprice of a lot of officers? And are there no pubs?"

"Only down in the town. This is a residential district. If you go, you will have to take the bus, and when you get there it will be closing time."

"It wouldn't be worth it," said Eleanor quickly, lest she might be left to the washing-up.

"Ladies' night!" cried Julia in a fury. "It sounds like a lot of red-faced Masons with wives in royal blue satin and pink carnations. 'We will put aside our secrets and our stories about copulation and give the old girls a break.' I couldn't go to one of those. My pride wouldn't allow it."

Eleanor, whose evening dress was royal blue, leant forward and said to Roddy: "What time do you start in the morning?"

"Nine."

'If I had Roddy,' thought Eleanor, 'my greatest happiness would be to go out with him to meet the other wives. Why should her pride not allow it?' She could not forgive Julia for wanting more than her own dearest dream.

"I wonder how long we shall be in this house?" mused Julia.

"For the duration. I've told you, you needn't worry," Roddy said. "I won't be posted now."

"The war might go on for ten years," said Julia, who was depressed beyond words. "Oliver might grow up to be a man in this funny place." She looked at Mrs Lippincote on her wedding day as she was often to look at her in the future. Nothing of her security, in these days. What would she have said to this? No home of one's own, no servant, no soup tureen, no solid phalanx of sisters, or sisters-in-law, to uphold her; merely—she glanced at Eleanor—merely an envious and critical cousin-in-law.

"Mrs Lippincote said she would call round at the end of the week," said Roddy, who had made the arrangements about the house.

"Oh, it is too bad!" cried Julia. "Is *she* always to be running in and out? To see if I have dust on the mantelpiece and . . . and to see if I am using the best china on a weekday. Which is the best, anyhow? It is all abominable."

"This would have cost the most," Eleanor said helpfully, picking up her bread plate and looking at the back of it.

"Oh, I daresay, we have yet to find the best and second-best," Julia said. "That corner cupboard will be filled to overflowing with it."

She got up and tugged at the green silk-covered doors of the glass cabinet. They creaked and came unstuck. Rows and rows of wine glasses shone in the sudden light, some with red stems, some with yellow, cut and coloured and frosted—champagne, port, liqueur, and brandy ballons.

"Jesus!" said Roddy, a little scared.

"Is there an inventory?" asked Julia, when she had turned the key.

"No. No one would take it on. God, I don't blame them."

"I was thinking I'd take all the ornaments from the

mantelpiece and bureau and lock them in the cupboards, but the cupboards are full."

She went to the bureau and opened the drawers one after another. All full: knitting-needles, playing-cards, paper-patterns, photographs (she foresaw a pleasant hour with those), some black-edged visiting cards and letters.

She felt burdened by Mrs Lippincote's possessions. "We shall never make a home of this," she cried.

"I wish you'd come to see it before you moved," said Roddy, reasonably, but uselessly. Eleanor concurred.

"But it sounded so nice," said Julia. "Big, and a lot of work, but cheap. And the plan you drew gave me such a pleasant picture of it. I imagined it all sunny . . ."

"So it will be," he said, and added: "On sunny days. It can hardly be sunny at this time of the evening and at this time of the year."

"It is not as if it were damp or anything," said Eleanor.

"It *is* damp," said Julia, "the kitchen is very damp." She felt at bay against the calm and decision of the other two.

"But we don't have to sit in the kitchen."

"Servants used to have to."

She felt suddenly exhausted, not knowing where to turn, or which was her worst enemy—Roddy or Eleanor or the house or Mrs Lippincote. Tears, as hard as bullets, pressed against her closed eyelids. She clapped her handkerchief to her face and fled from the room.

Roddy sighed, not from embarrassment, for Eleanor was his cousin and, living with them since war began, had seen Julia in tears more than once before; not from embarrassment, but annoyance.

Eleanor raised her eyes to the ceiling. "Over-tired," she said, as she might have spoken of a child.

"We are all tired," said Roddy gravely.

" I thought," Eleanor went on, with satisfaction, " I
thought it was only spinsters who behaved in that neurotic
way." She was forty and unmarried, she had a little money
in Imperial Tobacco, a royal-blue evening dress, and was
in love with her cousin, for whom, as they say, she would
have laid down her life with every satisfaction.

CHAPTER 2

OLIVER DAVENANT did not merely read books. He
snuffed them up, took breaths of them into his lungs, filled
his eyes with the sight of the print and his head with the
sound of words. Some emanation from the book itself
poured into his bones, as if he were absorbing steady sun-
shine. The pages had personality. He was of the kind who
cannot have a horrifying book in the room at night. He
would, in fine weather, lay it upon an outside sill and close
the window. Often Julia would see a book lying on his
doormat.

As well as this, his reading led him in and out of love. At
first, it was the picture of Alice going up on tiptoe to shake
hands with Humpty Dumpty; then the little Fatima in his
Arthur Rackham book, her sweet dusky face, the coins hang-
ing on her brow, the billowing trousers and embroidered
coat. Her childish face was alive with excitement as she put
the key to the lock. " Don't ! " he had once cried to her in
loud agony.

In London, he would go every Saturday morning to the
Public Library to look at a picture of Lorna Doone. Some
Saturdays it was not there, and he would go home again,

wondering who had borrowed her, in what kind of house she found herself that week-end. On his last Saturday, he went to say good-bye and the book was not there, so he sat down at a table to await its return. Just before the library was to be shut for lunch-time, he went to the shelf and kissed the two books which would lie on either side of his Lorna when she was returned and, having left this message of farewell, made his way home, late for lunch and empty of heart.

If this passion is to be called reading, then the matrons with their circulating libraries and the clergymen with their detective tales are merely flirting and passing time. To discover how Oliver's life was lived, it was necessary, as in reading *The Waste Land*, to have an extensive knowledge of literature. With impartiality, he studied comic papers and encyclopaedia, Eleanor's pamphlets on whatever interested her at the moment, the labels on breakfast cereals and cod liver oil, Conan Doyle and Charlotte Brontë.

This first morning in Mrs Lippincote's house, he buttoned his vest with his blue fingers (Jane Eyre), and thought he would take a look at the neighbourhood before a typical Lowood breakfast of burnt porridge and unclean milk.

His bedroom faced across the playing fields of a girls' school, not an encouraging sight in the morning nor, indeed, at any hour of the day. A line of leafless poplars appeared above the close boarding of the fence. Netball posts waited like gallows; a white pavilion stood at the edge of the dew-or rain-silvered grass.

It was Lowood, though, which blocked Oliver's vision, and which excluded this depressing vista of damp grass and peeling white paint. He sat on the bed swinging a sock, savouring the new and pleasing fact that he had come to live in a house with a tower. In a way it was nothing—neither ivy-mantled, nor filled with bells and bats and owls. Yet since his father had sent the plan of the house, he had

15

dreamed of it. Outside, it was a little feeble, not very hig[h]
and in good repair, yet had its gilt weather-vane as was rig[ht]
and proper. Inside, it was firstly a part of the drawing-roo[m,]
then half of his parents' bedroom, then an attic, locked b[y]
Mrs Lippincote, and the key held by her. Here, she store[d]
her clothes for which there was no room at Saint Winifred[']
View Hotel. It is acknowledged, however, that we none o[f]
us speak the truth about the rooms which we keep locke[d]
and Oliver was not dissatisfied with her explanation. He ha[d]
last night in bed, decided to put this room to his own us[e]
and there now, above where Roddy and Julia still slumbere[d]
he could distinguish the shrieks of Mrs Rochester flingin[g]
herself against Grace Poole in frenzy. He had come acros[s]
many odd and appalling conditions in his reading, drunke[n]
ness and hunger, jealousy, brutality, but this madness o[f]
Mrs Rochester's was his most formidable experience as ye[t]

He tied his shoe-laces in double knots and clanked dow[n]
stairs.

"It's only Oliver," said Julia, turning over in warm swee[t]
ness at the edge of a dream.

Eleanor was swung ruthlessly from her hammock of slee[p]
'That boy!' she thought. 'If I had a son, I'd . . .' She wa[s]
gone again, trying to recapture the dream in which she ha[d]
sat lunching with Paul Robeson in the Savoy Grill to sho[w]
the world the quality of her moral courage and her indiffe[-]
rence to its colour bars.

Oliver crossed the dark hall and peered through th[e]
coloured glass of the front door, first at a ruby, then a purpl[e]
then lastly at a sepia world. Then he opened the door upo[n]
the grey-and-white, early-morning, spring-chilly Sain[t]
Winifred's Crescent. Dead it looked, like the photograp[h]
in a newspaper of a road where murder had been committe[d]
Oliver was not especially appalled by all the gables an[d]
spotted laurels of the other houses. He had never foun[d]

himself in congenial surroundings and now looked at it all as if it were a description in a book, which bored him, but which he was not compelled to read. In this way, he walked with indifference down the wide pavement where a tree or two grew at the kerb, examined little notices at tradesmen's entrances, saw several crocuses on rockeries of clinkers and the sour hard earth in shrubberies. Who has not walked in a madness of oppression down such roads? At the corner was a large house with glimpses of white furniture at bed-room windows and a brass plate at the gatepost—that Saint Winifred's School, to which the white pavilion belonged. That was the end of the Crescent. There it opened out into the wide main road, where buses ran, where there were more schools, some nursing-homes, doctors' houses, and cricket fields; no shops, nor, as Julia had been warned, public houses. It was a district where whistles and the punt of balls and the savage roars of people watching games would depress one and force one thankfully indoors on raw winter afternoons.

Some lettering on a green wooden board caught Oliver's attention. He stood by the fence and read, ' Sunnybank Preparatory School, Montessori Methods.'

It was not what he had imagined. The name ' Sunny-bank' (for this was the school Eleanor had decided on for him, where she herself was to teach) had given him some idea not only of the sunny bank itself, but of there not being a tree in sight. This house was smothered in trees, even now before the leaves were completely unfurled. There was no bank, no sun. A few browning snowdrops withered bleakly on a rockery, or clinkery; there were monkey-puzzle trees, pampas grass, a conservatory full of deck-chairs, a rustic summer-house and all the rest of the paraphernalia. He had no idea what Montessori Methods might be, but hoped that Eleanor would see to it that it was not some foreign system of torture or coercion.

He stood at the gate and sent his spirit (or rather Jane Eyre's) forth to inspect the house. When he was convinced of it all, the smell of it, how the doors opened, which way the stairs went, and in which room he would have the Montessori thing done to him, he turned back towards home. He was tired already and hungry, and if Mr Brocklehurst were coming, why then he might be made to stand on a stool half the day, with a placard round his neck and no food in him.

． ． ． ． ．

Breakfast was very little better than supper of the previous evening. Julia had not yet settled down, Roddy supposed, as he squashed sardines into a silvery mess on a piece of toast. After this, there was bread and butter and egg sandwiches left over from the train and from supper. He sighed and went on duty.

"I went to see the school," said Oliver.

"And what do you think of it?" Eleanor asked.

He took a curled-up sandwich. "Well, it isn't very nice, is it?" he said, as kindly as he could.

Julia lit a cigarette and picked up Oliver's book from beside his chair. "I haven't read *Jane Eyre* for years, have you, Eleanor? There's something about those girls that gives me the creeps."

"What girls? Oh, Brontë girls!"

"Once I saw Emily's comb, a very nasty-looking comb, too. She dropped it off the horsehair sofa the moment she died and it fell on the fire. Charlotte grabbed it, which seems an odd thing to have bothered about doing with her sister dying. There it is to this day, a bit burnt. One of the most horrible things I ever saw."

"I thought she died standing up," said Eleanor, beginning to stack up the breakfast things. "I thought it was a thing they went in for, like standing up for 'God Save the King'."

18

"You are turning into a mad little bookworm," Julia said to her son, having whetted his appetite a little further. He thought that every time his mother opened her mouth she said something which interested him.

"Before you begin school, I think it would be a good idea if Eleanor gave you a few sums each day; or some tables to learn," said Julia vaguely. She had never learnt tables herself and consequently gave them an importance they could not deserve.

Eleanor had gone to search for a tray. "There's a corporal at the back door with a parcel," she came to tell Julia.

"Is a corporal a high-up kind of officer?" asked Julia, patting her hair before the mirror, and feeling anxious to do Roddy no disservice with his superiors.

"He is not an officer at all," said Eleanor scornfully. "And I should not have left him standing on the back door-step if he had been."

Julia found what she thought 'a nice lad' waiting with a parcel in his hand. He straightened up stiffly to resist the charming way in which she tried to console him for not being an officer. "With the Wing Commander's compliments," he said, his eyes steadfast over her shoulder and fixed on the plate-rack above the sink in an unnerving way. He saluted and disappeared.

Inside the parcel was a neatly trussed chicken and a little package with its windpipe and giblets. This inspired Julia for lunch, at least; so that Roddy came home to something better than he had had reason to expect.

"A darling little boiling fowl," said Julia. "It was thoughtful of him. I could have done with it half an hour earlier, though."

Roddy looked pleased. Whether it was with the Wing Commander or the boiling fowl, Julia could only guess.

"I wonder if you would like to come round to the Ante-

room for a drink this evening, if Eleanor's staying in," Roddy suggested.

"That would be nice," said Julia. She realised that now, having no life of her own, all she could hope for would be a bit of Roddy's, what he might have left over and could spare.

Since Roddy had made the suggestion, Eleanor felt she would be quite glad to stay with Oliver, and write some letters.

"I should like to meet this kind Wing Commander," said Julia. "Now, he really is high up, isn't he?"

Eleanor, who thought this vagueness about rank an affectation, looked sideways at Roddy.

"He is the boss, my dear," said Roddy, with simple devotion, so that Julia half expected him to cross himself.

Eleanor thought what a splendid thing it would have been for Roddy to have had some woman behind him to make his career her life's work, and to be an inspiration and incentive to him. 'To understand him, in fact,' she added grimly for her own benefit. 'That is what spinsters in books are always thinking about other women's husbands.' She tried not to behave like a spinster in a book. Her sense of humour saved her, she believed. She put up a good fight and fell into only the less obvious traps, but she bothered a little more about her dignity, and her position, than do the majority of married women, and betrayed herself by what Roddy called her 'little ways', by which he meant the trivial comforts, consolations, cups of tea and patent medicines, small precautions against draughts and a gentle fussing which grows insidiously upon and characterises those who have neither husband nor children to cherish and only themselves to put first.

As soon as tea was over, the desolation of Sunday afternoon began to disperse. Julia, who had meant to lie down

after lunch, found she had passed the afternoon perched uncomfortably on the arm of a chair going through, with calm unscrupulousness, Mrs Lippincote's bureau. Roddy, who had been carefully brought up and would not have done this for the world, very sincerely protested, and Eleanor who had intended to look through the photographs but probably not the letters, as soon as she was alone, protested, too. Neither of them would glance at the treasures Julia kept discovering. Oliver was lying on a shelf in the conservatory reading.

"Oh, not the letters!" cried Roddy.

"Cards first," said Julia, who descended one by one the shelving levels towards absolute (she hoped) intimacy.

"I am ashamed of you," said Roddy, who obviously was. "You are behaving like a housemaid."

"Housemaids behave no worse than other people," said Julia.

"It is a question of education," Roddy shouted. "Education leads us forth into adult life, where prying and spying just do not happen."

"Yet I was educated," said Julia. "I went on being educated until I was eighteen. Why did it work with you and not with me?"

"It must have been a very bad school," said Roddy, who had thought so once or twice before.

"I cannot get this quite straight," his wife complained, laying out black-edged visiting cards as if she were beginning to play patience. "Who is Lady Fennester? She must have been a widow for years and called on Mrs Lippincote a great deal. Is this she in the spoon-shaped hat and her neck bandaged with a silk scarf?" She peered at a photograph. Neither of the others showed any interest, even when a yellowed newspaper cutting with an account of the wedding established Lady Fennester's identity—'The bride's mother

in brown parchment watered silk and toque of clustered velvet parma violets, with brown veil.'

"Oh, I should have known." Julia took the small photograph up to the large wedding group and compared them. "So her people were titled. I suppose she must have married beneath her."

"A title is nothing," said Eleanor.

"But a title is everything. It goes a long way. And makes the world of difference."

"You wouldn't care for Mrs Lippincote to know you've rummaged in her desk, would you?" said Roddy.

"Of course not," she replied. "She must have looked splendid. All these dresses were champagne georgette and lace, Eleanor."

"Really?" said Eleanor. "What time shall we have tea?"

"Oh, God! it's four o'clock already," and Julia, without artifice, bundled back all the cuttings and cards into the drawer. "Letters another time. Look! The children on a sheepskin rug—Leslie, Colin, Leonard and Phyllis."

But no one would look. So they had tea. And after tea, there was Oliver to get to bed and Julia must change, and Eleanor spread out her writing things on the dining-room table to write to 'my friend, the Prisoner of War.'

Roddy and Julia walked along the Crescent on their way to the Mess. At the Saint Winifred's View Hotel which they passed, Julia slackened pace and gazed at the array of tumblers, water jugs and table napkins at one of the two front windows. "Perhaps Mrs Lippincote sits at that table," she suggested to Roddy.

He was now in a mood to indulge her, and smiled, standing himself a little out of range of the window, farther up the road.

A church, and then a chapel, dribbled out a few people

on to the pavements outside. They lingered, in little knots and clusters, by the railings. Roddy picked a piece of cotton from Julia's shoulder and led the way into a requisitioned hotel, where another scrubbed-looking corporal stiffened up and cast over himself the mantle of impersonality. Julia thought her husband increased in grandeur as he entered the building. He opened a door and she was shown into a large and pleasant room with wicker furniture and a bright fire, a few officers and a great many ladies drinking gin.

"How nice!" cried all the ladies, with false *bonhomie*, as Julia was introduced, and the Wing Commander himself, a sardonic man who leant against the mantelpiece doing his wife's knitting, bent over and took her hand.

"Now, Harry, don't drop your stitches!" cried the wives of senior officers. He loved that, Julia could tell. No wonder, then, that he approved his officers having their wives in the town.

"Thank you, for . . ." she began, but he held up the knitting at her in a silencing way, and Roddy cast an anxious glance in her direction.

Conversation was desultory. Julia thought that some focal point was missing, for the women were restless and chatty, twirling gin glasses and sending quick looks at the door, the clock, or diving, with no apparent result, into their handbags. Presently, she realised that some of the husbands were missing, were playing snooker; sometimes an emissary would arrive from them, order drinks, hover awhile at each abandoned wife and disappear.

The evening was going forward—not smoothly, but with little jerks and creakings, sighs and backward glances. Julia pondered on this while she talked to the Wing Commander's wife about butchers and laundries.

Eleanor's evening, on the contrary, slipped into smooth waters at once. "My very dear Reggy," she wrote, without feeling any surprise whatsoever. She had not known Reggy well nor cared to know him better when he had gone overseas four years before, and had begun to write to him—"Dear Reggy"—simply because it was in her anyhow to be a prodigious letter writer. Then he was killed and she found that, barring Roddy, he was all she had to offer up for her country, and wept. But after a month or two, he was not killed, but a prisoner-of-war. In her relief, he became "My dear Reggy". It was obvious that she was still only a short way up that scale which culminates, one supposes, in "Darling", "My Love", "My Own".

She wrote her letter, signed it "Your E", wrote on the envelope that monstrous word *Kriegsgefangenenpost*, and put it proudly on the mantelpiece. Then she sat down by the fire with a rather bogus book about China, and fell asleep. As soon as the first Mrs Rochester had quietened, Oliver fell asleep, too.

.

Eventually, the husbands, and life itself, returned. They came back rosy with pleasure, squaring their shoulders, rubbing their hands and ordering drinks.

"Now Roddy will have to cover up his tracks," they teased Julia. She smiled as readily as she could, but had no fund of back-chat for them. The Wing Commander, amid shrieks of protest, began to turn the heel. The party was beginning.

The women, already a little reckless, let their handbags slide unheeded to the floor, looked no longer at the door and obviously not at the clock. A young officer began to play the piano. Most of the songs the men hummed loudly, or sang with various words slurred over, looking at one another in a solemnly wicked way. The women smiled, as mothers smile at their indulged children.

24

At eleven, the Wing Commander left, gathering up knitting and also his wife—who still recited the names of grocer, doctor, dentist and dairyman at Julia—and curtly and austerely went from the room.

Then chairs were moved back, the party collected round the piano, and a few women began boldly to sing.

" *Now* Roddy must watch his step."

" *Now* we shan't see much of him."

Suddenly, Julia felt herself illuminated by the gin. She put her hand in Roddy's and smiled.

"There's the girl!" they cried, thinking she was nice, really, but shy.

Her vitality seemed to lift her on her toes, her head spun round like a planet. In her happiness she began to blossom and unfold. She even tried to join in singing a rude song, but Roddy soon put an end to that, shaking her elbow gently until she came to her senses.

Around midnight the party disintegrated, and Roddy and Julia walked back along the deathly Crescent. Eleanor had left sandwiches for them.

' It is better,' thought Julia, looking round the room, ' than last night. It is already more of a home.'

She knelt on the rug, with a sandwich in each hand.

"Enjoyed yourself ?" asked Roddy.

"Oh yes! I shall never get up in the morning. How gay we are going to be. What fun you must have been having all the time I wasn't here," she said accusingly. She stood up and brushed crumbs off her skirt into the fire. " *Kriegsgefangenenpost* ", she read from Eleanor's letter, and sighed for her and then, beginning to go upstairs in the darkness, sighed for herself as well.

"Tell me," said Roddy, "whom do you love ?" He put his arms round her waist.

She knew he thought her to be slightly drunk, as indeed

she was, and that, in the circumstances, he hoped to wrest some secret from her.

"I love myself," she said lightly. Then, reaching the landing and remembering Mr Lippincote, she leant her head for one second against him. "And then," she added, "miles down the scale, in a vague, bewildered way, I love *you*."

Then he knew she was truly drunk.

CHAPTER 3

JULIA HAD a strange gift of coming to a situation freshly, peculiarly untarnished by preconceived ideas, whether of her own preconception or the world's. Could she have taken for granted a few of those generalisations invented by men and largely acquiesced in by women (that women live by their hearts, men by their heads, that love is woman's whole existence, and especially that sons should respect their fathers), she would have eased her own life and other people's.

She did not—probably never would now—realise that generalisations are merely conveniences, an attempt to oil the wheels of such civilisation as we have. It is exhausting to come newly to everything, to have the same decision to make over and over again.

One of Julia's non-beliefs was that, since we are no longer creatures in a jungle, a father must surely concern himself in his children's health with as much concentration as the mother. This had often led her to thinking how strange and detached Roddy was. She had read articles on mothercraft in which the father was quite ignored, but dismissed this as

journalism. "I leave it to you, dear," Roddy would say. "I leave it to you completely."

Eleanor, who had not seen more of the world, but had drawn some conclusions from what she had seen, implored her often to leave a few details concerning Oliver's temperature and digestion until Roddy had finished supper.

"But he would wish to know," said Julia. "A chill on the liver is a very tricky thing and the first news I should want when I entered the house would be to know how Oliver had been. And Roddy the same. You don't understand how much like fussy old hens parents can be."

"Roddy knows that if anything were to go wrong you would let him know at once."

"He wants to be reassured."

Yet Roddy, taking off his hat and smoothing the red line it had left on his forehead, seemed apathetic about Oliver's bowels. "Yes," he said tiredly. "Good. That's better."

"Aren't you going to see him?" she asked, for he had turned towards the dining-room.

"Isn't supper ready, then?" He hesitated, and then went upstairs.

Oliver sat up in bed eating arrowroot mould. He wore one of his father's white school sweaters. 'Davenant' was embroidered in black letters across the chest and back. 'Dav' started off large but the letters trailed off, growing smaller and crowding into the arm-hole.

"Hallo, old man."

Oliver took another spoonful. "Hallo."

"Had a good day?"

"Yes. Thank you."

"What are you reading now?"

"*Rainbow.*"

"Is *that* still going? Good God, not that vile girl, Bonnie Bluebell, still?"

Oliver nodded, looking with more interest than usual at his father. Roddy picked up the comic paper and glanced through it.

"What did you do to-day?" Oliver asked him.

"Good heavens! Paula and Peter. Marzipan the Magician. Mrs Bruin. Scarcely altered at all. Eh? Oh, I gave some lectures."

Oliver nodded again. His face looked narrow and exhausted, his eyelids heavy. As he pushed aside the plate of arrowroot, Roddy, with sudden love and compassion, noticed the thinness of his little wrists, the flatness of his forearm lost in the wide sleeve.

"Poor old chap." He touched the warm dry skin of his forehead with his lips. "Anything you want?"

"I'd better have the pot. I feel sick again."

"All right, old boy. I'll fetch your mother." He went downstairs two at a time, calling Julia, and clutching the outside sheet of *Rainbow* in his hand.

At supper, Julia said: "Well, that's finished Oliver for starting school to-morrow."

Eleanor was looking forward to her new job beginning the next day, and was not sorry to be unencumbered by Oliver, for the start.

"Just for a day or two," she said in an encouraging way.

"He's kept scarcely anything down," said Julia, fetching a medical book from a shelf. "'Liver. Biliousness'," she read. "Would you say Oliver's is a febrile condition, Roddy?"

"Hardly."

"Oh. 'Fever. Night sweats. See Tuberculosis.' Oh, heavens! Page 885." She flopped over the leaves. "How horrible this book smells. 'Tuberculosis. See Consumption. Page 239'." She flopped back again, took a forkful of curry and began to read. Then she closed the book quietly and

28

went on taking little forkfuls of rice with her head bowed. When Roddy saw a tear or two drop on to her plate, he got up (he had just finished) and came round to her. He put the big book on the shelf again and kissed the top of her head.

"Don't be silly, darling," he advised her.

She laid down her fork and began to cry. "I can't bear it if they take him away from me."

"Why should they? Who is 'they'?"

"Those dreadful sanatoriums." ('Sanatoria' thought Eleanor, eating quietly). "I can't help remembering that horrible book I once read called *The Magic Mountain*. I couldn't bear Oliver to go there."

"You and Oliver both read too much," said Roddy, self-righteously. "Why on earth should . . .?"

"It just describes him—how hot he gets in bed, and that cough he had at Christmas, and his paleness and prolonged irritability."

Eleanor took a second helping.

"But, Julia, if I look up—Saint Vitus' Dance, or—or duodenal ulcer, you will find he has those, too. It's a well-known fact."

It was nice of him not to laugh at her or try to jolly her into good sense.

"I see." She blew her nose and began to collect up the plates. Eleanor, who was either a bit greedy or phenomenally hungry all the time, had just laid down her fork.

Julia fetched in the custard tart and ate with as good a grace as she could manage, but anxiety had lain down inside her, and as she sat darning after supper, she fetched deep worried sighs up from her lungs.

Roddy fell asleep in his chair, as he so often did, and looking at his pink, round, rather babyish face, she felt no irritation towards him, only tenderness. 'Dear Roddy,' she thought. 'How could I manage without him?'

Outside the window, the new leaves on the trees were all ruffled one way by the wind. The sky was bitterly white behind them.

Her love for Roddy persisted while they drank their cocoa and went up to bed. With a feeling of suspense, she opened Oliver's door. He was sleeping quietly with his arms thrown above his head, fingers curled to the palms. On the pillow beside him, he had placed a little cobra made of green and yellow plasticine. It was curled in a spiral and reared up its flattened hood. Its eyes were the two halves of the aspirin she had given him to take with his Bengers'. His forked tongue was one of her hairpins, which often scattered over his bed when she kissed him good-night. The sight of the little plasticine snake quite tore from her heart the tendrils of anxiety which had grown there as she read Mrs Lippincote's *Home Nursing Encyclopaedia*.

She was her normal self when she joined Roddy in the bedroom. He stood in his shirt, and suspendered socks, taking a stud from his collar, looking, she could not help thinking, less like a lover than a husband.

"O.K.?" He grinned.

"Yes," she said shortly.

When he emerged from his shirt and began to scratch his back, he said: "Big Church Parade on Sunday."

"Oh, yes?" She was suspicious at once.

"It pleases the Old Man enormously if the wives sometimes show up."

She looked sternly at him, as she kicked off her shoes. "Roddy, my dear," she said coldly. "I have no particular objection to arse-creeping, but I will not do it in church."

He realised that her worries about Oliver were for the time-being over; she no longer needed him to sustain her.

They finished undressing in silence.

Oliver's patience, when he was ill, was almost disconcerting.

"The child's a born invalid," Roddy would say, for he could not forgive his son's having grown up more quickly than himself. And he was disappointed. He did not see Oliver's essential toughness, nor realise that thin wrists can be like steel. He could not be sure that he was going to be good at games, nor even that he would want to be.

The child wanted very little amusing. Julia went through Mrs Lippincote's library, which was hidden nicely behind greenish glass doors, and found *The Wide, Wide World*, *Little Lord Fauntleroy* and *A Peep Behind the Scenes*. She fetched a basket of leaves and twigs from the garden and an old tray, and Oliver embedded a miniature green wood in plasticine and lay back on the pillows looking listlessly at it and, having diminished himself to the size of an ant, walked coolly through the green reflecting tunnels and stared up at the brilliant light raining down through the veined leaves.

Julia's struggle with the house was a hopeless one from the beginning. It was too big for them, and the charwoman, dividing out her labour among her 'ladies' as if she were handing round a plate of scones of equal size, could only manage to come once a week. Mrs Lippincote, having found this inadequate, had been driven to Saint Winifred's.

At nine on Fridays, Mrs Whapshott arrived with her rolled-up apron in a basket, and Julia, who had been up early to dust the more obvious and horizontal surfaces of furniture, would then shut herself in her bedroom and smoke, for the woman made her nervous. From the beginning, she had put Julia in the wrong, for Julia confessed she saw no reason why they were especially lucky to have Mrs Whapshott on a Friday. "To get set straight for the *week*-end," the woman said, putting the stress that way. "But we never do anything much different at the week-end," Julia persisted,

31

PICKERING PUBLIC LIBRARY
CENTRAL BRANCH

thinking that the drift of all this was that she was being asked for more money. "You have your husband at home, I expect," Mrs Whapshott said sternly. So Julia was afraid of her and dreaded Fridays. She also looked on Mrs Whapshott as a spy and imagined how the slow but sure disintegration of the house was being reported to Mrs Lippincote at the Saint Winifred's Hotel.

The disintegration of the house resulted from neglect, from the accumulation of jobs to be done to-morrow. Cupboards and dark corners there were which Julia avoided, which she felt she never could clear out. For the first week, daily expecting Mrs Lippincote to call, she had thought the excuse of having just moved in would cover most deficiencies, but Mrs Lippincote had not come and the excuse which was dead was needed more than ever now. When a bell rang she would look up at the glass panel in the kitchen and see with some relief 'Side Door' wildly agitated. Sometimes it was the Corporal, who would turn up unexpectedly and yet with fatalism, in the manner of a soothsayer in a Greek play, arriving with the compliments of the Wing Commander and an invitation, or a cauliflower from his garden, or a note from Roddy, perhaps, to say he could not be in for lunch. Once it was a covered basket in which lay a great ginger hare, dead, with its nose in a tin bucket and blood on its fur. Julia, lifting the piece of sacking and thinking it was a dead cat, had suddenly screamed, and the Corporal had lowered his eyes from contemplation of the plate-rack and smiled at her.

Each day Oliver ate a little more arrowroot mould. Julia made it every way she could think of—white (vanilla), brown (chocolate), pale-brown (coffee) or just pink. Sometimes, layers of all these and then she was late with the lunch.

In spite of the way Julia gummed up his inside with

nourishment, Oliver remained thin. "Gone away to nothing," Mrs Whapshott said cheerfully.

Eleanor, whom he did not really like, set sums for him every morning and corrected them when she came home for tea. Occasionally, he had a right answer, in much the same manner as when one backs horses a great deal, now and then one of them comes in for a place.

When Eleanor had shown him his mistakes, she would tell him how pleasant life was at Sunnybank and that she could not remember having taught in a school with such a nice atmosphere. Miss Cowper and Miss Threlfall he tried to imagine, and asked a few questions intended to supply the bare facts he needed, and not to encourage Eleanor. He was left with a picture of a large raven which was Miss Cowper, and a wintry little robin which was Miss Threlfall. But Eleanor's tongue was running on and she had to stop short of saying 'Threlly' by braking so suddenly that her voice skidded. After all, Oliver would one day be a pupil, so 'Threlly' would not do at all. He listened to her against his will, as they say condemned men cannot help themselves from looking out through the grating at the brick wall, their butt and journey's end. When she had gone, he would turn it over in his mind—the other children with their smart answers in class, then what Eleanor called the 'equipment', particularly the frames where one learnt to do up buttons and tie bows, the sand-trays and the reading cards. He would have to sit in that class, he was told, for arithmetic and writing. As for reading, he would certainly be needing no cards. For that, he would be with the bigger ones. He picked up *The Wide, Wide World* and took another look at the little girl in the white stockings. He was falling in love again.

When Eleanor went downstairs she could hear Roddy and Julia talking in the little conservatory. He had just come in and bore the red hat-mark across his forehead. It was stuffily

33

warm and dusty there. They were musing over an early wasp which Roddy was shortly to kill, though Julia did not know that and would ineffectually protest when he did. It had shaken itself free of a piece of cobweb, which already contained a few dead flies, and now went through a kind of ancient ritual, bowing and stroking its great antlers (they were watching closely) with its crossed forelegs.

"What a monster he is!" said Julia, and it was then that Roddy squashed it and Julia said, "Oh, no!" So she punished him by reserving some pleasing information until she had finished stacking up a pile of flower-pots according to size. Then she said: "The Wing Commander's wife came in to see Oliver this afternoon."

"That was very decent of her."

"Yes. They had a good talk about *The Wide, Wide World*. I think it is the only book she ever read, so it was lucky."

"What do you think of her?" asked Roddy.

"She twitters. Like all the wives of sombre men, she froths and seethes and bubbles, keeps herself at boiling-point ready for emergencies."

Roddy did not like that quite so well, so he changed the subject. "I went into the Grand at lunch-time, with Edwards, the one who plays the piano. And met an old friend of yours."

"Oh, good!" she said. "Who was it?" She had not before realised her loneliness, her love of London.

"Yes, a strange coincidence." Roddy looked teasingly at her. "You remember the man who ran La Belle Charlotte?"

"Mr Taylor!" She hid her disappointment, hating being teased.

"I expect London became uncomfortable for him. I always thought him crooked."

She considered that, and seeing the wasp drawing his body into an agonised curve, knocked it off the shelf and stamped

on it. "I never thought him that," she said. "Except that he has the kind of conceit which sometimes seems to turn men into murderers."

"Well, his conceit must work overtime now. He is down in the world indeed."

"Yet staying at the Grand."

"Staying is right. In a white jacket, serving drinks in the Lounge."

"A white jacket?"

"Oh, yes. It was very white. I'll give him that. The same grey suède shoes, too. Wait until to-night."

"No," she said slowly. "I can't go to see him doing it. That I can't. Did he see you?"

"We had a chat. He said he was bombed out of Soho. Sheer terror, I suspect," said Roddy, who was brave. "He asked if Madame was well."

"What did you say?"

"I said 'Yes'. You are, aren't you?"

"And you told him that I am here? In this town?"

"I don't remember. Oh, Eleanor, your friend from Frith Street is working at the Grand."

"*My* friend!" she cried, coming in and fanning at the stuffy air. She, unlike Julia, enjoyed being teased. "That horrible man!"

"I thought you admired him, and his wide shoulders and nice shoes," Roddy lisped. "I thought that was why we must always in those days eat in Frith Street."

"Oh, it was for Julia," said Eleanor. "They fascinate her."

"They?"

"You know what I mean."

"I suppose he was obsequious to you," Julia suddenly broke in. Roddy would have liked being recognised by some-one deferential from London when he was with his friend.

35

She suddenly moved away and went upstairs to change. They had arranged to meet Edwards and a woman officer for dinner at the Grand. While she was peeling off her stockings she decided not to go and also (it was not quite the same decision) that she could not leave Oliver. Eleanor, knowing how Threlly would like to hear about it in the morning, went in her place.

When they had gone—Eleanor pretending that she was unaware of Roddy's displeasure—Julia read for a little to Oliver, but she felt languid and inclined to yawn. *Little Lord Fauntleroy* did not amuse her nor interest her in the least. She was easily sickened by stories of pretty widowed mamas and their little sons. She picked up Oliver's arithmetic book and gave him a little talk on the value of mathematics. He lay propped on one elbow and listened with her own amount of enthusiasm and the same number of yawns. Then she went downstairs. The darkness was beginning now to hold away from the evenings and there was a period of neutral colouring and undecided light in which a few birds sang and sounds like buses starting up on the main road, steps along the pavement, or rain (and it was often raining) were magnified and isolated. The house was shadowy, and full now of ticking clocks, the stairs creaked and popped, and wardrobes exploded suddenly. She had nothing to do. Mrs Lippincote's bureau held no interest for her. It would have been sordid to have pried into it when she was alone in the house—a strange nicety which Mrs Lippincote herself might not have appreciated.

She wandered out through the front door and walked miserably among the shrubs. She could imagine how wretched it would all look on late Spring afternoons, so much golden privet and laburnum against the bright red walls. At the back of the house the paths were edged with curly rolls of terra-cotta. Great snails with patterned shells had

36

silvered the tiles and the tongue ferns and the new cone-like leaves of the lilies of the valley. At the end of the garden among the rhubarb leaves and pieces of broken cucumber-frame was a miniature gravestone on which were carved the words:

'Fenella, A Faithful Friend. Aged Twelve.'

Julia sat on a seat under a pear-tree and watched the light fading out from between the newly-leaved branches and, as it receded, the house standing forward in a more solid and menacing outline. She considered the evening before her and wondered at what time they would come home. She could not think why she had not gone herself, especially as she was frightened always of being in a house alone. Sometimes, she thought, that it was this thing, this one terror, which forced her to endure Eleanor's living with them. It was safe enough sitting out here in the garden, nothing could harm her, but in the house, with the light beginning to fail, there was always the fear not of the room in which she sat but of the other rooms where she could not be and which, once it was dark, she could scarcely bring herself to visit. Eleanor laughed at her, but she was not completely ashamed, knowing that none of us are without our blind unreasonableness, either pride or fear or both. Yes, she wished she were sitting now at the Grand—drinking coffee, were they, by now? It was not that she had expected to be stimulated by the company. Women officers habitually condescend to civilian wives, and, as for Edwards, he was harmless to the point of imbecility; but she suspected him of altering his accent according to the company in which he found himself and anyone who will do so will be found a poor and timid companion, hedging conversation round with little anxieties and agonies, so that each time he mentions a fashionable restaurant or good wine or an important friend a solemnity is given to the occasion, as if a flag is planted and unfurled.

37

Heads are bowed and one wonders how on earth the conversation will struggle to its feet again.

Julia, sitting under the pear-tree, considering men and their small idiocies; and conscious all the time of life burgeoning in the branches above her, of the sap rising and all the imperceptible movements among the creaking buds and the gropings of cramped and folded leaves, suddenly became conscious, too, of a white curtain fluttering in the topmost window of the turret. The curtain waved like a palely gloved hand and she stared at it with extraordinary fascination. It was the only room in the house to which they had no key, and the window had been closed before.

She realised, then, how long she had been sitting beneath the pear-tree. The light had been finally withdrawn and now she must cross the lawn and enter the house in an almost complete darkness. Had Oliver not been there, she would have walked the streets until Roddy came home, or gone after him to the Grand in her darned cardigan, rather than go inside that house. She called to Oliver in a subdued voice, standing beneath his window, but there was no answer and she supposed he had fallen asleep long before. She walked quietly in through the front door and stood in the hall, trying to sense any change there might be, but could detect none.

She stood there, with the blocks of shadow which were furniture on all sides of her, and felt the waves of sweat break regularly on her body. At last, her ears straining above the confusion in her blood, she heard a key slip with an oiled sound in a lock, and then quick light footsteps down the carpeted stairs. Without hesitation the steps crossed the wide landing and a young woman in a white coat appeared. She was bareheaded and carried a suitcase. She came hurrying downstairs and before Julia thought she had been seen, she heard a high, ringing voice bidding her 'good evening'.

The waves receded suddenly, leaving her limp and weak. She put out a hand towards the hall table to steady herself. "Who are you?"

The young woman came up very close to her, closer, Julia thought, trying not to recoil, than was either natural or necessary.

"I am Miss Phyllis Lippincote," she said, with a smile of dreadful conventionality.

Julia waited. Miss Lippincote swung her case.

"Did you get what you wanted?" Julia asked, at last.

"Oh, yes." She looked round the hall, swinging her case, rocking from heel to toe, shoulders hunched up as if she were cold. "Yes, thank you." Again she flashed at Julia that social smile.

"I wish," Julia tried to say, "I wish I had known you were here. I was rather frightened when I saw from the garden that the window had been opened."

"Nothing to be frightened of," she was assured. "It does the room good to be aired sometimes. Well!" she sighed again with conventionality, and sauntered towards the door.

She shot out a thin damp hand and shook Julia's and swung away down the drive.

'Heavens!' thought Julia, watching her go. 'How she frightened me. What an unfortunate first meeting! She will go to her mother and tell her I am mad.'

She went upstairs to bed, since there was nothing else to do, and lay yearning for the sound of Roddy's and Eleanor's voices on the drive below. It was after eleven when she heard them, and by then her unsociability had been well punished. They had had quite a time, they told Julia, sitting one on each side of the bed. Quite a time! Rocking with laughter they were, and she shrank from the smell of alcohol as do those who have not been drinking and wish they had.

" Miss Lippincote called," said Julia, when she could get a word in.

" Oh, grand, I'm glad you were not alone," said Roddy taking up her hand and squeezing it and not noticing that it dropped back on to the pillow. His eyes met Eleanor' continually, for they could see in one another still the reflec tion, a glimmer, of the gaiety of the evening.

" What about Mr Taylor? Did you see him? " Julia asked coldly.

" Oh, no! His evening off, I think. Eleanor was so disappointed."

" I see," Julia cut into his cousin's protestations. " Well now, I think I'll go to sleep," she said, moving her legs in the bed so that she nearly tipped Eleanor on to the floor. They went stumbling and giggling in search of some food. " Blood is thicker than water," Julia decided. " Even cousin blood."

CHAPTER 4

THE NEXT DAY Mrs Lippincote herself called. Julia was shopping, and Oliver, climbing from his bed and thrusting his head out of the window cautiously, saw the top of a black straw hat on which, apparently, a swan had alighted and a long rolled umbrella poking at the gravel. When he had decided that it was no one with whom he wanted to converse, he crept, without a single creak or rustle, back into his bed. Julia found the card when she returned. She put down her basket and examined the card carefully as if it would presently reveal some secret, until she noticed drops of thick blood running from the shopping bag. The *Daily*

Worker (for Eleanor now veered towards class-consciousness under the influence of a visiting carpentry master) is an admirable newspaper in many ways, but for wrapping up any meat other than imported pork it is entirely inadequate. When she had unstuck the liver from the racing news, she sped upstairs to Oliver. The black and white hat described as it had been seen from above enchanted her.

" Did she knock more than once ? "

" No. Only once."

" Or look in at any windows ? "

Even Oliver felt that this would have been an unsuitable thing to do and smiled as he shook his head.

" The *Daily Worker*," cried Roddy at lunch, for Julia's description of Mrs Lippincote's visit must be led up to by every detail of circumstance or emotion. " How could the *Daily Worker* have got into this house ? "

Julia pointed her knife at Eleanor and went on eating. " One of Eleanor's funny little papers," she said, when she had finished her mouthful.

" Oh, no ! " said Eleanor, who had found one glance at Roddy sufficient. " It must have been changed at the butchers."

" I always take my own newspaper," Julia pointed out.

" I don't like to have our meat wrapped up in other people's newspapers," said Roddy, meaning ' in newspapers which have probably been read by the working class.' But Julia had filled her mouth again and Roddy did likewise.

" The meat can always be washed," said Eleanor.

" No. Makes it tough." Julia was gobbling because she wanted to rush out to the chocolate soufflé. " Never wash meat," she said warningly, as she pushed back her chair and ran to the kitchen. Eleanor had a headache to-day and wished she had stayed at Sunnybank for lunch. She felt uneasily that Julia might have been prying in her room, as

41

she pried into Mrs Lippincote's bureau, or how else had she come by that paper? It was not that she had anything to conceal, but that she had nothing to conceal. As it was Mr Aldridge's afternoon for carpentry, she left her coffee and hurried away.

Roddy scraped the paper inside the soufflé dish with a spoon. "We ought to give a little party one night," he said. "A house-warming party. Then the boys can sample your vol-au-vents."

Julia melted at that. Cooking almost always fired her imagination. "As soon as Oliver is quite better," she agreed. She wondered whether crab or mushroom.

"Both," said Roddy grandly. "Are you any happier here now, love?" When she could not answer, he sighed.

"Oh, I am hopeless!" she said impulsively. "I find it so difficult to be happy. I wish it were not so. Are you happy?"

"Yes, on the whole, I am very happy. I suppose this life suits me, interests me."

"What would interest me, suit me, I don't know. I daresay I want life always to be pleasure—sitting in the sun, drinking."

"Pleasure is not happiness."

"No." But she still saw herself beneath a striped awning, at the edge of some pavement, a market square, and its cobble-stones full of shadows and high lights like a tubful of suds. On the iron table a glass was still clouded with some frosted drink, there was the smell of sun-baked foreign newsprint; warmth, leisure, delight, relaxation, the frosted drink an illumination of contentment at the back of her head; across the table a shadow leaned forward and laid a hand over her hand on the iron table.

'It is no table I shall ever sit at. I shall go on regretting that until I die, or (and she was honest and knew that it was desire which had ridden high in her at that moment) until

42

I am forty or fifty. The shadow is something I have cast myself.' And she looked up and there was no shadow, only Roddy fallen into a doze with an empty cup in his hands. 'Men and women are not always the same,' she thought. She was sorting this idea out for herself, as if it were the first time it had ever occurred to anyone. 'We spend half our lives driving ourselves frantically against a brick wall in our agony for something which if we took we should despise. They—they fall asleep and so renew themselves, since to be sought so passionately so—devilishly—must exhaust them.'

Roddy opened one eye then the other. "This won't buy the Sunday dinner," he yawned. "What are you thinking, with your chin in your hand?"

She sighed. "I was thinking . . . that I am nearly in the prime of life. Oh, curse it!"

He laughed. He stretched, smoothed her hair, glanced in the mirror and went off, still yawning, to earn the Sunday dinner and defend his country.

.

Mr Aldridge was a little lame and had a kind of waxen beauty. Miss Cowper was harsh with him, but Threlly could not be harsh. It was in her nature to mother him, as she mothered all the children. "A *born* mother," parents said approvingly, and then, with sadness, "What a pity it is!" But who can be sure, since born mothers so often turn out dismal failures when faced with their own offspring, forced to watch the frigid, the pleasure-loving, the indolent romping away with their children's affection, while they themselves sit at home with the darning basket?

Eleanor, dismissing her class from the workshop at four o'clock, liked to stand there among the shavings talking to Mr Aldridge. He was doing some work of his own, a little carving—Aphrodite rising from the sea. It was practically

only the torso of a girl and a crest of wave in beechwood. She looked, not dewy-eyed with surprise like Botticelli's achievement on the same lines, but rather smug at having kept her hair dry. Eleanor, whose opinions about art were often a reflection of what she thought of the artist, would not allow herself to recognise this. She watched Mr Aldridge rolling up his tools in a canvas holder, gouges and chisels with handles of rosewood and boxwood.

Threlly brought in a tray with tea. Through the open window they could hear Miss Cowper clapping her hands among the departing children, settling a dispute. "It's my Jesus book, you little liar!" Then the hands clapped furiously, a child wailed from temper and the injustice of the world and they could hear Miss Cowper crying wildly, for it was the end of the day and the week: "Children! Children!" At last they were all gone, and Miss Cowper came into the carpentry shop, worn to a rag, she said. She pushed back her dark hair with both hands, and drank her tea. "Why *here*, Threlly? I like it, though. Peaceful. Oh, thank God for *tea*!"

It charged them all with gaiety. Eleanor took two spiral shavings and fixed them on either side of Threlly's face so that she looked like—who? They could not quite decide. Miss Matty, perhaps.

It was natural that Mr Aldridge should walk back towards the Crescent with Eleanor, for his lodgings lay that way along the main road towards the town itself. Eleanor tactfully developed a long, slow-swinging lope to keep time with his shuffle and drag.

'He needs a good woman to care for him,' Threlly thought, watching them set off. Eleanor called back: "I shall be bringing my Oliver along on Monday."

"Dear little fellow," Threlly murmured, nodding and smiling.

44

"You know," said Eleanor in a low voice to Mr Aldridge, "he is not really a dear little fellow at all."

"Little boys so seldom are. How old is he?"

"He is seven. But very backward."

"Does he always go to the school where you are teaching? Doesn't that make things difficult for you?"

"I have not been teaching since war began. I've been ill, and living with my cousin and trying to help in the house."

"I'm sorry. I hope you are better," he said politely.

The slow shuffle and lope was conducive to confidences. "I had a breakdown," she began. "It sounds vague, but it isn't pleasant nor vague. One thing after another—voice went, and then, when I recovered that, alopecia—that means one's hair falling out in great patches." Her hand went up to the back of her head in a nervous gesture. "Then neuralgia, insomnia, loss of memory."

"You must have had some shock?"

She hesitated. "Yes. Look, the lilac trees are in bud!" she cried with bright artificiality. She tried to resist the temptation, struggled and failed. "My—a dear friend was reported missing, then killed, then, after a long time, a prisoner of war."

"Your fiancé?"

She hesitated again, then said firmly: "No."

"It was nice of you to tell me," said Mr Aldridge.

"Oh, I am ashamed of myself. Other women go through all that and worse and never turn a hair," she said contemptuously.

"Other women? Some women, perhaps, but not all. Some, like you, suffer."

But she wished to be alone in her suffering and did not answer. For the rest of the way, they discussed politics, deplored the absence of the Second Front, and Eleanor, for

the first time in her life disloyal to Roddy, told the story of Julia and the liver and the *Daily Worker*.

.

Mrs Whapshott, having discovered that the week-end was less important to Julia than it had been to Mrs Lippincote, transferred the benefit to one of her other ladies and came to Julia on Mondays, with the understanding that she would do no washing.

On the first of these Mondays, Julia went in to Oliver to call him to dress ready for school. His clothes lay spread out on the window seat—vest, pants, grey shirt and shorts, red and white tie, red-topped socks, red snake belt. Oliver himself sat up in bed grinning with a rash as thick as porridge over his face and neck. For once, Julia did not run for the Medical book. She knew.

" Oh, Oliver! " she cried. " How could you! "

So Oliver slid down into bed again and waited for his breakfast, lying there contentedly, working on one of his loose teeth, but with apathy for, although each pulled tooth was exchanged for sixpence, Julia and he had allowed this childish magic to become mercenary and commercialised, and he had been advanced threepence on this particular tooth some days before, on the security that it was hanging by a thread. " You might as well give him a lump sum for the whole set," Roddy had grumbled to Julia. " What do you want with them, anyway? "

Julia telephoned the doctor and folded the school clothes, and Eleanor went off to Sunnybank alone.

" It's one thing after another with children," said Mrs Whapshott. " I remember with Madam, if it wasn't chicken-pox it was the scarlet, or dip. And she had the four."

" Madam's—I mean Mrs Lippincote's daughter called the other evening," said Julia.

"Oh, Miss Phyllis!" Mrs Whapshott gave a curious and baffling laugh and said, well, she had better leave Oliver's room for the time being what with the infection. 'Miss Phyllis!' she repeated to herself. She smiled and went up to do Eleanor's room, the only tidy one in the house. She did not complain, for life was upside-down for everyone and Madam living in a boarding-house, but 'officers' wives!' she sighed as she went upstairs. 'We certainly have to meet all kinds these days,' she reflected.

.

"No reading!" said the doctor, taking the book from Oliver's hands and drawing the curtains half-way across the window.

Oliver and Julia both stared at him in horror. He touched his own eyes. "Ought to know that," he said. "A very nasty complication with measles. Better a few days than all your life." He placed the stethoscope against Oliver's blue-veined ribs and tried to concentrate, while Julia chattered wretchedly. "How could he have caught it? He hasn't moved from that bed." She flung out her hand dramatically. The doctor looked at her in a jaded way as he wound up his stethoscope. 'Officers' wives!' he, too, was plainly thinking.

In the afternoon, Julia sat down with her knitting and a copy of *Kidnapped* which she began to read to Oliver with an enthusiastic Scots accent, running sometimes into a Rhondda Valley lilt, or at others into a sly County Cork drawl. When she could read no longer, they played cards. Lying back in her chair, she watched Oliver's thin hands dealing out the cards with slow deliberation. "Oh God, make him fat!" she prayed. "Please God, if only you would, I'd believe in you. For ever and ever, amen." As she picked up her bundle of cards, her mouth smiled, but her eyes flashed and swam with tears.

47

The front door bell rang just as she was thinking about getting tea. Looking out through the window, she could see the Wing Commander wiping the inside of his hat with a handkerchief, then the back of his neck, then replacing his hat on his head. She hooked up her skirt fastenings, hesitated by the mirror, and ran downstairs.

From the hall, she could see the violet and yellow shape of him through the glass door. Having seen him mopping himself a moment before, she could forgive him easily the manner of dark silence in which he entered the house.

" Well? " he began at once, " aren't you going to offer me tea? "

The answer to that is a dipping curtsey and a graceful gesture with the bell rope. Who would respond? she wondered and looked up at him and smiled. He thought it was a strange smile and said so, in a raised voice, trying to remember if she were deaf, seeing in her expression the willingness to hear of those who cannot.

" If," she began, looking in an absent-minded way into his hat which lay on the hall table, and noticing that it came from hatters in Sackville Street—' As I was going down Sackville Street' she thought. Not the same one, though.

" If what? "

She lifted her face and gave him one of her rare smiles, quite different from the other. " If you had a long cloak " (her hands described it for him) " and whiskers," (she laughed) " then you'd be Rochester to the life. And Oliver would think so, too. Are you trying to be he? " (He is too old, though, she thought.)

" You impertinent . . ." he began, but something checked him before he could say ' baggage '. ' Junior officer's wife ', he thought. " Who is Oliver? " he asked gravely.

" My son, who is upstairs on his sick bed. Would you like to let him see you? "

48

" Upstairs? "

" Yes. Sir," she added, " have you had measles? "

" Measles? Naturally."

She followed him upstairs. Oliver flattened his card house and then looked up.

" Dear, it is Mr Rochester to see you."

A faint flush went up Oliver's cheeks.

" I will talk to your son while you get tea," said the Wing Commander. " Just a cup. Nothing to eat." In his inmost mind, he had thoughts which delighted him and would continue to do so when they recurred in the future. " Roddy'd have a fit," he told himself. " She must be an anxiety to him in some ways."

When Julia came back with the tray, he and Oliver were playing Beggar My Neighbour rather listlessly and in silence, eyeing one another uneasily in alternate glances over the cards.

" So you read Charlotte Brontë? " the Wing Commander asked condescendingly. He sat on the end of the bed sipping weak tea. Oliver ate cornflour mould.

" Yes."

" Called that stuff ' shape ', when I was a boy. Children like it nowadays. We never did. My daughter, Felicity, chooses it for her birthday pudding." His manner, even when speaking of cornflour mould, was menacing.

" Felicity is a pretty name," said Julia, hoping it was apposite. He knew she was thinking that. Yes, Roddy'd have a fit.

" *Jane Eyre* is NOTHING to *Villette*," he observed.

" No. *Nothing*." Julia leant forward with her hands clasped on her knee. " Oliver has not yet got at *Villette*."

" When I was a boy, I went to see that place—Pensionnat Héger. In the Rue d'Isabelle. Yes, it was all there—the Berceau and the Galérie. I walked up and down the Allée Défendue. You remember? "

" Ah, yes! Describe! "

" The front of the house a flat façade built right on the pavement with rows of long windows, and all round—new buildings towering above, scaffolding, heaps of rubble, one side of the Pensionnat torn away. They were demolishing it," he said, turning to Oliver. 'These two pairs of eyes fixed on me,' he suddenly thought.

" Go on," said Oliver's lips, through which no sound came.

" That was where Charlotte and Emily went to improve their French. All alone, very proud. Brave girls." He held out his cup for tea and Julia poured it quickly and carelessly. ' He is not Mr Rochester any more,' she thought, ' He is just himself.'

" I don't believe it is not there any longer," she said. " Either it was never there, or it is there still. One or the other."

" It was pulled down many years ago. Before the last war."

' That makes him at least . . .' Julia tried to reckon, moving her fingers secretly in her hair as she began to add up. He watched her for a little while, then he said: " I am forty-nine."

" Oh! " She looked up in relief. " Yes, you could be that."

" I *am* that." He was back at Mr Rochester again.

" My mother saw Emily Brontë's comb," said Oliver, nodding at Julia.

" Darling, we mustn't boast. It was nothing. Oh, it is true, but anyone might see that. No one can see the Pensionnat Héger any more. It is sad how things change. It is sad and sickening."

" Have you been to see the Abbey Ruins? " he enquired. They shook their heads.

" Take the boy when he's better. You really should. Penny

50

ride on the bus, that's all. Go past the gas-works and it is down by the river, just beyond the prison."

" It does sound heavenly," said Julia.

" Yes, well worth a visit." He shook hands with Oliver and followed Julia downstairs. He picked up his hat and stood looking at it for a moment. " Goodbye," he said in his most sombre voice, and walked with overwhelming majesty from the house.

" The old man," cried Roddy at supper. " Good God. What on earth for?" He was profoundly disturbed.

" For tea, I think."

" Good Christ!" He tried to imagine the scene, but could not. She helped to sketch it in for him.

" On the *bed*! My dear Julia! Did Oliver behave?"

" I think we both behaved," she said kindly, guessing that it was what he really wanted to know.

" Gracious heavens! What did you talk about?"

" We talked about Charlotte Brontë."

" Charlotte Brontë!" He breathed the words as if he were in a dream. " Charlotte Brontë!" He shook his head. " Good Christ!" he said again. " Good Christ!"

CHAPTER 5

NEXT FRIDAY, Mr Aldridge, feeling that it was Eleanor's turn to listen, invited her to a cup of tea at his lodgings. The house was in Mozart Terrace, a façade of crumbling lavender stucco and iron verandahs behind a row of chest-nut trees, which had shed their sugary pink blossom into the dust.

51

Eleanor resented the landlady's welcome. She thought her falsely cheerful, as if she were dealing with invalids and as if she were trying to imply that it would be taken for granted that all relationships with Mr Aldridge were innocuous. She turned the little outing into a sick visit, instead of tea with a bachelor in his rooms.

"Do women cherish all men who limp, however slightly lame they are?" Eleanor wondered, trying to discover in Mr Aldridge some likeness to Lord Byron, but failing.

In the room where they awaited tea, flimsy french windows were closed against the verandah at the front of the house, and through an archway and at the far end of another room, a laburnum tree, a mass of fading fawn-coloured blossom, swayed against the glass of another garden door. The draught occasionally lifted the edge of the carpet.

Eleanor thought it would have been pleasant to have sat by a fire, but the dark grate contained merely a fan of crinkled paper. The moulded garlands on the mantelpiece were the faintest impressions beneath layers of thick whitish paint. Much of the fretworked furniture was white, too, or had been at some earlier date. It was a room to cast a chill over all who entered it. A plain and well-made bookcase was filled with rows of undusted and apparently unread Left Book Club volumes, the *Communist Manifesto* and *Origin of the Family*, the *Ragged-trousered Philanthropists* and a book on Grinling Gibbons.

The landlady brought in the tea, smiled at them as if they were good children having a dolls' party, playing nicely on a wet day, and left them alone.

Eleanor liked pouring tea and handed cups as gracefully as an Edwardian hostess. When this business was settled, she relaxed in her chair, hoping the warmth of tea would soon invade her body and prevent her teeth from chattering. Mr Aldridge did not seem to feel the cold.

"This is nice," she said hopefully.

He could not eat naturally. It was no use. Each bite he took from the accursed macaroon biscuit seemed to split the room in two, and if he let it rest a little in his mouth to soften, the ensuing munching was still unnerving. Hungry as he was, he trembled with frustration and stared out resentfully at the dusty chestnuts and the dull afternoon sky. A sultry breeze had begun to ruffle the leaves and swirl a little dust round, as a prelude to rain. No, thank you, he would have no more tea. Eleanor regally poured some for herself. Now cigarettes! This was better. Smoke softens the air and the stiff line of the mouth can be hidden.

"And these are all your Bolshy Books?" Eleanor asked, going down on her knees at the bookshelves, her eyes narrowed against the smoke from her cigarette.

He had winced a little. "I should like you to meet some of my friends in the Party," he said, wondering whether he really would like this. Eleanor was prepared to meet anyone.

"I have to keep my . . . activity to myself," he told her. "My job, you know . . ."

"But, surely, Threlly would never object?"

"It might make it difficult for her with the parents."

"How could a Bolshy carpentry master make any differ-ence?" she asked in her innocence.

"It might," he said stiffly. "And then, you see, there are my classes at the Grammar School."

"I see. There are some things which never occur to those of us who are outside. We go on thinking we are in a free country and that everybody else is expressing himself as he pleases."

Mr Aldridge now saw himself as martyred, victimised, sacrificed. Perhaps he was, if it is true, as we are often told, that our integrity is our most valuable possession.

Suddenly he said: "Not that it makes much difference either way."

Still kneeling on the carpet, she looked up in surprise. "Why? But why?"

He picked up *Grinling Gibbons* and stared at a glossy plate as if he could neither understand nor see the pattern of vine leaves, oak leaves, roses and ears of wheat. Then it seemed to become clear to him. Tears were ready to spring to his eyes at the beauty of it. "It is really not interesting to anyone but myself," he said, with steady modesty, "but a shock to me, naturally. The doctor has told me I have three months to live."

"Three months!" cried Eleanor, as if she could have comprehended four, or six, but not three. We can all remember saying something inadequate in a crisis or even, the more unbalanced of us, giggling at the news of death. Everyone confided in Julia; in Eleanor, no one, as a rule. She had no knowledge of how to meet the occasion, sitting there with a book called *Fallen Bastions* in her hands.

"Oh, no!" she said at last. "I refuse to believe it." It was the easiest, not the noblest, way out. "Don't *you* believe it. There's a time limit on all our lives, but the flavour goes from them if we acknowledge the fact. I just say to myself that I am going to live for ever, and if the thought of my own death comes to me in the night, I turn my mind to other things. So you must do the same, d'you see? It isn't true. It-just-is-not-true." She banged her fists down on the book and when she raised her eyes, she saw sadness and pity in his. "What are you going to do?" she asked in a different voice.

He closed the book and stood smiling at it. Then he shrugged his shoulders. "Nothing. At first, it was like being young all over again. I thought I had so little time left I must do something great. But you don't. You do nothing.

54

You go on exactly as if you did not know, and all the time you are waiting for the grave, just as one always is whether one knows how long or not. When the time comes, of course, I'll be sorry, regret this, that and the other, wish I had done many more things, but that's how death must come to everyone. Only for the very few and the very old can it be any different."

" You are very brave."

" Yes," he said honestly. " I seem to be brave. That surprises me very much. I always thought of myself as rather a coward ! "

" Who can help you? " she cried. " I can't. It seems impossible even to think of the right things to say."

" To help me you must promise never to try to think of the right things, nor hope to avoid the wrong ones."

" Who else knows? "

He blew a little dust from the top of *Grinling Gibbons*, and put it back in its place. He shook his head and smiled at her and the landlady came in for the tea things. As she was stacking up crockery on the tray she clicked her tongue in annoyance, for they were naughty children now, and had not eaten enough.

" I must go," said Eleanor, scrambling to her feet.

She walked back along the gritty pavement feeling overwhelmed. The spring seemed to have become smudged and rotten, the trees dully bluish green, railings coated with dust, lilac dead, laburnum dead, guelder roses dying, pink may was a little sickly, white may quite overpowering. From the playing fields a solid click at intervals, but no noise. No whistles in the summer. She passed ochre-red tennis-courts. A girl in white swung up her arm and crashed balls into the net. As she crossed from side to side her face was red, impossible to tell whether from anger or exertion. Coolly-dressed people sat on the edge of the pavilion, bouncing

their rackets on their toes, and smoking to discourage gnats. A bus went by heavily, its tyres licking the tarry road.

Eleanor rounded the corner by Saint Winifred's School and heard with nostalgia—for her own schooldays had been entirely happy—a bell ringing for supper or preparation or for evening prayers. She listened to the voices of girls, and their footsteps on the stairs, and envied them.

When she reached home, she found Oliver up for the first time. He sat at the dining-room table with a sum book opened before him and a paper dart in his hand. He laid down the dart as Eleanor came in, and sighed. Julia sat on a stool drinking gin and water. "A vile drink," she said to Eleanor, perhaps in explanation for offering her none. "Have you been to tea with your young man?" Her very way of saying 'your young man' implied that he was not, and was not likely to be, anything of the kind. She always dealt too lightly and therefore cruelly with Eleanor's personal life.

It is seldom safe to confide in lonely people. Their very loneliness requires the importance of making known the confidence, at hinting at its existence and source, if not actually divulging it; better to trust in busy, popular people, who have no time for betraying one and no personal need to do so.

Julia was tied to a wide circle of people by their secrets, almost as if she were a maypole with her ribbons in a multitude of hands. Her own fallibility drew others to her. No ribbons streamed out from Eleanor. What Julia took lightly she, Eleanor, prized highly.

Mr Aldridge's confidence meant too much to her, and out of pride, not treachery, she let his secret fall into Julia's hands. Julia laughed. "Don't believe it, Eleanor," she advised. "When chaps say that, it is never true. Like people who threaten to commit suicide. He is probably trying to

orce you into something out of pity." She glanced at Oliver's
back and grimaced.

'Oh, God, give me back those words!' prayed Eleanor.
Poor Mr Aldridge! Would no one, then, believe in his
imminent death? She herself had brutally denied it to him.
And yet more brutally boasted of it to Julia.

"What is wrong with him then?" Julia went on.

Eleanor hesitated. It had never occurred to her to ask him.
"I have told you too much already," she said.

Julia finished her gin and Eleanor went upstairs.

Oliver fingered his dart and sighed again. "I feel tired,"
he complained.

"You'll sit there till you've finished," his mother said
unsympathically.

Oliver pushed away his dart and rested his cheek on his
hand. "Two sevens are fourteen and another is . . ."

"Look," said Julia, reaching for a scrap of paper. "You
know two sevens are fourteen. Quite correct. Now you want
one more. Suppose, then, that it's two you've got. Another
fourteen." She wrote down the two fourteens and a couple
of lines underneath. She paused. "Well, actually I think
it would be easier if you learnt your three-times table."
Irritably, she began to write it out for him.

"Here's the sun, now," said Oliver, gazing out at the
privet clumps. "And I'm missing it all!" He made seven
dots, counted them up and wrote down the answer. "I
sometimes wonder if you want me to be strong. Three and
three is six and six is twelve and ten is twenty, I suppose. Or
delicate all my life . . ."

"Will you be silent?" Julia slammed down pencil and
paper and stood up. "Sometimes, Oliver, I think I shall
end up in a lunatic asylum."

"Yes," he said politely. He waited a respectful second
and then put out his hand towards his dart. She suddenly

smacked him. He sat with his head bent, blinking hard. "
beg your pardon," she said haughtily. "Take your boo
to Eleanor and ask her to be good enough to correct wha
you've done. And another time try to be not so tiresome."

She went to the window and dabbed at her eyes. "Th
whole business about bringing up children," she explaine
to herself rather self-righteously, "is to know when to los
one's patience."

Upstairs, Eleanor seemed to be opening and shutting on
drawer after another. The floor above creaked and vibrate
The telephone rang. Roddy would not be home until late.

"Well, then," said Eleanor, coming downstairs and striv
ing to show she had forgiven Julia. "We can manage wit
some cheese."

"Why? Why? How did this notion get round that wome
cook only for men? Why, indeed, should we manage wit
some cheese, just because our—our sexual organs ar
different?" Julia stormed.

Eleanor sat down on the bottom step and giggled weakly
One way and another, the day had been too much for he
When he heard his mother joining in, Oliver paused in hi
teeth-brushing and listened. He loved to hear Julia's lon
loud, rippling laughter.

"'Sexual organs' sounded grand," Eleanor wept, "yo
are getting to be quite a lady."

Julia went happily to the kitchen. They managed wit
some cheese.

CHAPTER 6

" YOU ARE getting to look like Robert Louis Stevenson,"
Julia said anxiously.

Oliver glanced up in interest and pleasure.

" You must have your hair cut, and we shall see what that
will do."

" Will you come with me, then? "

" But, dear, I feel such a fool sitting there with all those
men staring at me."

" Just for the first time," Oliver begged. " Until I get
used to the new place."

She really did feel foolish, sitting on a bench waiting for
Oliver. She accepted a cigarette from the barber and took
up a crumpled newspaper. The barber was a Jew, with
heavy-lidded, Oriental eyes, his face sculptured into deep
folds. His expression, as he worked with the razor, was intent
and murderous.

Julia laid aside the newspaper. Steaming towels were
brought and draped over the customer's ('patient's' she
thought) face. The man—and she could see nothing of him
but the top of his head, a wave or two of brassy hair—lay
back luxuriously. Julia glanced at her watch.

There are few murder cases in the war-time newspapers,
but Oliver had found one.

Now the towels were removed and lotion was being
massaged in. 'Oh, men!' thought Julia contemptuously.
She could see dark roots to the brassy hair, or fancied she
could. She was more than willing to see them and to dis-
approve. The Jew unswathed towels from the man's wide
shoulders and he stood up. He was unusually tall. Julia met
his glance in the mirror. " Good morning, madame," he

59

was saying quietly. Julia at once recognised the suit. It was a very fine piece of cloth, but a little too much of a good thing across the shoulders.

" Mr Taylor ! " They shook hands.

" I'm afraid you've been looking at me in a very vexed way," he said. " I'm more than sorry to have kept you waiting."

" Oh, but could you . . . ? "

" I had a little peephole through the towels. I could see you in the mirror."

" Oh."

Oliver, who was nervous of the barber, climbed on to a high stool and looked reproachfully at Julia, who seemed to have withdrawn her support at the very moment it was needed.

" I met Flight-Lieutenant Davenant," Mr Taylor was saying.

" Oh yes, he said so."

" I had hoped to see you as well."

" My son has been ill." They turned to look at him, perched up on the stool in a long grey cape, bunches of his silky brown hair falling from him. He sat there, hunched up, brooding and outraged, rather like an eagle in captivity.

" It is a pleasant surprise seeing you, madame. It brings back the happier days—before the war," he added. When he smiled, she looked up into his face and was shocked. He was not growing old merely, he was collapsing. His face had folded into stern lines, his eyes were emphasised by the shadows beneath them, and his brow darkened by contrast with his hair. " It has done me good," he continued. " I hope it will happen again."

The barber's face was imperturbable. His lower lip curved moistly outwards as he combed and snipped. At last, he swept the cape from Oliver's shoulders, flicked it out, as if he were

a matador, and once more stood on one side, awaiting pay-
ment. Oliver—a very different Oliver—slid down and
grinned.

"Why, surely," Julia was saying. "I am sure to see you."
Oliver touched her elbow. "Goodbye." She put out her
hand.

"Goodbye, madame." It was like the old days indeed.
She might have been leaving after lunch, full of rather soggy
crêpe-de-volaille, and he bowing at the door, with regality,
not servility. Oliver pressed his fist against her side. She paid
the barber and when they reached the street there was no
longer any sign of Mr Taylor.

"Shall we go for some coffee?" Julia suggested.

"If you would like to," said Oliver, knowing well she
wanted to go, so refusing to have it regarded as a treat for
him. "Madame," he said.

Julia made a feint at him, which she changed into a wave
to an airman passing on the other side of the road. Roddy
had asked her to recognise (he had meant 'bow to') the
N.C.O.'s from his own squadron, and this was the best she
could do, to make sure, by remembering—one might almost
say 'accosting'—them all. This A.C.2 behaved as most of
them did; he half-stiffened in either surprise or surprised
horror and passed on quickly. "I am no longer in the least
attractive, then," Julia mourned. She had obviously missed
Roddy's point, a not uncommon happening.

Oliver skipped along, like a sheep relieved of the weight
of its wool. He had stopped looking like Robert Louis
Stevenson.

.

"You have not yet warmed your house, Davenant," said
the Wing Commander in the Ante-room. He held his beer
to the light, then he swilled it round and quickly drank it—

a time-honoured hint from old men in pubs, but not to b
regarded so among officers in the Mess.

" Same again, sir ? " Roddy asked.

" No treating, Davenant ! " He laughed sourly and place
his empty glass on the tray. " I put a question to you."

" Well, sir, there've been measles in the house."

" Measles is over, now. I myself saw to it." It was th
first time he had referred to his visit. Oblique as it was,
was a reference and Roddy waited for more and in vain.

" I think it could be arranged, sir."

" See to it. See to it. Your health, Rodney ! "

' Rodney' pleased very much, and palpably.

" Hard work this hot weather," Edwards murmure
behind Roddy's shoulder.

" What ? "

" You know," said Edwards.

CHAPTER 7

TO TIDE OVER for them both the awkwardness of their nex
meeting, their consciousness of time passing, Mr Aldridg
suggested a bus ride to the town to meet one or two of hi
friends. The streets were crowded, queues waited under th
striped awnings of shops, babies lay under canopies, preg
nant women sailed out of the clinic, the air glittered in th
heat. At the market-square, a narrower, meaner thorough
fare crossed the High Street ; this was the Vasco Road an
led to the gas works. Here, the shops were smaller and ther
were green-tiled pubs at corners and cafés with chalke
menus outside—faggots, tripe and onions, pigs' trotters, blac

uddings and other low-class foods. Flies circled over the
lum-coloured meat, the orange fat, and pallid sausages
ere looped across the windows. Dogs snarled from door-
eps, children fought and their mothers shrilly but ineffe-
ally interfered.

Mr Aldridge opened the door of a grocer's shop and
leanor went in. It was cool and dark, smelling of soap
nd bacon. Sawdust stuck to their shoes. An old man, who
as cutting a cheese, said 'good afternoon' and went on
ith his work. Mr Aldridge led the way up some stairs. At
ie top was a door with glass panels and a lace curtain across
iem. He opened the door and whistled and was answered
y a low groan from along the passage. In the front room
iey found a large man lying on a sofa stretching and yawn-
ig. "Hallo, Sarge!"

"Why, hallo, Chris. Feel tired." His face was blotchy,
is eyes stained with sleep. He yawned again, sat up, blinked
t Eleanor, stood up. Mr Aldridge introduced them. They
iook hands nicely.

"Sit down," said the man, Sarge. "Get some tea. Half
sec." He yawned and yawned.

"Don't bother for us," Eleanor began, thinking she would
ie if she got none.

"Must for Vera," he explained. Standing, he seemed not
) immense. He padded away in his stockinged feet and they
ould soon hear him moving round the kitchen, clumsily
ollecting together crockery, filling the kettle and lighting
ie gas.

Eleanor looked round the room—two sash windows there
ere, not clean, a fawn, characterless wall paper, a deal table
overed with a typewriter, a duplicator; then, the worn
ioquette sofa and an empty grate littered with cigarette ends
nd toffee papers. A breakfast cup full of faded dog-roses
ood on the mantelpiece and a large clock with a brass plate,

63

She got up stealthily to read the engraving—"To o⟩ comrades 'Sarge' and Vera Viney on their wedding da⟩ January 1, 1943. Steynes Branch, C.P.G.B."—and sat dow⟩ again.

"He is the Secretary," said Mr Aldridge.

"And where is his wife?" Eleanor whispered.

"At work. He is working nights and she is a dispense⟩ They meet on the doorstep and exchange greetings."

When Sarge came back, he had on a pair of white tenn⟩ shoes and had combed his hair. He made a space on the tab⟩ and set down the tray. As he was pouring out, they hea⟩ the shop-door bell ring and someone running upstairs.

"Vera," said Sarge.

She came in and let an armful of books slide on to t⟩ table. Eleanor she greeted coolly and taking her cup of t⟩ over to the window, "You are all yawning," she said, an⟩ flung up the pane. She put her cup and saucer on the s⟩ and leaned out, gazing down into the street.

'She is fine and beautiful but, by God, she's rude,' Elean⟩ thought.

Sarge was talking to—yes, she must accustom herself ⟩ thinking of him as Chris. He had many of those litt⟩ mannerisms which either repel or please us in a publ⟩ speaker according to whether or not we agree with what ⟩ is saying. Doubt would materialise on his face with a frow⟩ would be harried this way and that in a fit of blinking an⟩ dismissed finally with a sniff. Then he would run a fing⟩ thoughtfully down his nose or pull the lobe of an ear. Elean⟩ watched in some fascination, but on the whole witho⟩ managing to understand what he was saying, since the⟩ appeared to be talking in initials. Vera, who had no dou⟩ seen it all before, leaned out of the window and sipped h⟩ tea. A different facet of Chris was now exposed, neither th⟩ maiden lady's treasure nor the doomed invalid, which we⟩

all she had seen before. Death ceased to be his only claim to importance, as he sat there eagerly reeling off his initials— E.C., T.C., E.P.T., T.U.C., C.P. At school the little boys would say: " That's a tashing knife ", or " What a flop of a conker ", and the mothers would smile warmly at one another. Eleanor smiled warmly to herself now with Chris making a speech about the I.L.O. and something he had found out from the L.R.D., and Sarge listened respectfully, curling his ear lobe in his fingers until it was bright red.

Eleanor examined the titles of books on a shelf near the fire—*The Communist Manifesto, The Ragged-trousered Philanthropists*, some Left Book Club editions, *The Origin of the Family* and a book on Birth Control.

Vera became animated suddenly, leaning far out of the window and calling to someone down below. She turned and flicked her fingers impatiently at Sarge. " Kirsty's forgotten her key. Shop's shut." Sarge—it was his turn to be talking and he did not pause—pulled a bunch of keys from his pocket and threw them to her—Vera, with a pleased smile, closed the window and came back to the table to fill her cup. Eleanor tensed herself unconsciously to meet another stranger, or more? she wondered, hearing a voice on the stairs. Kirsty was young, a little Scots girl with freckles, and the man who followed her into the room towered above her.

Vera waved her hand vaguely at them—" Kirsty. Leo. Eleanor." When Leo clicked his heels together and bowed stiffly, Kirsty sighed and shook her head at him. Leo said nothing. He looked tired. His old jacket had a foreign cut.

Now Sarge was listening to Chris. He did this with as much concentration as when he talked. Not till Chris had finished, did he look up and say: " Hello, Leo. Get that article done? " Leo handed him a packet, drank his tea rapidly which he could do since it was now tepid, clicked

his heels and left them. As he passed Kirsty, he clasped his hand over her long red hair and half-circled her neck. She put back her head in sensuous recognition, as a cat will when stroked.

"I shall have to go," Eleanor found courage to say. Time had passed quickly while she sat there listening and observing.

There were no polite protests, but Sarge said "Come again!" as he shook hands. "Yes," Vera murmured, standing very straight beside him. She slipped her hand in his and her fingers whitened. 'She wants him to herself,' Eleanor thought.

Kirsty had taken off a shoe and was gloomily damping a little ladder in her stocking. "Oh, goodbye!" she said cheerfully.

Once through the dark little shop, there was much to discuss. Chris, too, thought Vera cool almost to the degree which is arrogance.

"She loves Sarge madly," was the most he could say. "He is a very fine person."

"She is a woman of—education?" Eleanor suggested.

"Yes. A very clever woman."

"And Sarge—has he always worked in that factory?"

"Lord no! A great many other factories as well," he laughed.

"I see."

They climbed into the bus. "Vera's determined. She meant to have the best and she got it. Sarge is a very fine chap," Chris said once more.

"And this Kirsty, and Leo? Where do they come in? Are they married? Engaged?"

"Oh no! They just live there. They are nothing at all to one another."

'That is where I think I know more than you,' Eleanor thought. "He is a very silent man," she said.

66

Chris fringed the tickets solemnly. "He would be, you see," he explained. "He is dumb."

"Oh!" Eleanor felt shocked and embarrassed. "You should have told me before we went. It might have been—appalling."

He thought this over. "It wouldn't have been," he said simply. "But I didn't expect him to be there."

The High Street had changed. Shutters were down and windows covered with dark blinds. Shadows had lengthened. The mothers, the pregnant women, the prams, had given place to young girls strolling in twos, soldiers and a few French matelots.

"They all look different, yet each one is typically French," said Chris.

"Why 'Sarge'?" Eleanor asked suddenly. "What an odd name for him to have. Why?"

"I don't know," said Chris. "I've often wondered, but never liked to ask."

The bus shuddered once more to a standstill. "I've enjoyed myself," said Eleanor. "I hope we may go again."

CHAPTER 8

JULIA WAS making flaky pastry. Oliver liked to sit watching her folding in lard, rolling, folding, turning. The quick movements of her strong wrists, powdered with flour, pleased him. Mrs Lippincote's old mixing-bowl pleased him, too. The creamy glazed earthenware was scribbled over faintly with sepia cracks, and a spiral of indigo wound thickly round it. He was probably the only person who had ever thought

67

it beautiful. Julia stamped out the centres of the vol-au-vent cases and took the baking tray to the oven. She knelt there, sodding and blasting with the heat puffing over her red face, and brought out another tray of pastry. " Risen beauti-fully," she told herself. She began to clear up and Oliver returned to his arithmetic book. " Nine and nine is eighteen," he began to drone. Roddy had said he shouldn't go to school until the next term, but get his strength up instead, run wild a bit. Oliver simply didn't know how to run wild, so he sat in the kitchen and watched his mother. And five is twenty-three.

Julia was laying tea on the kitchen table, the loaf and knife, a pot of jam, a couple of Crown Derby cups and saucers, and two white plates with gilt clover-leaves in the middle. When she had made the tea, they drew up their chairs, bent their books backwards to prevent the pages from closing and then propped them against jug or tea-pot and began their tea. When they had eaten and read for some time, they closed their books and began to stack up the tea-things.

" I still don't make out where babies come from," said Oliver, when he closed his book, *Tess of the d'Urbervilles*. " Oh, where *from*. I know that. But not how *that* began."

" Oh," said Julia. " I see. Well, now," she assumed an expression, controlled her mouth. A flat and unemotional tone, she had read once in a pamphlet on sex-instruction. He wondered what was wrong with her voice. " This bores her," he decided. She sounded unutterably fatigued. " It bores her more than anything else in the world." Julia, busy draw-ing on the back of an envelope, seemed to be conveying a wrong impression and leaving out the most important part. She had never been good at drawing and had in any case only a hazy idea as to how such things are arranged. Bladder, then some loopy tubes, glands. ' It looks like a picture of a Sheraton chair,' she thought, discouraged. Half-way

through, curiosity made her give a glance at him. His gaze slanted down away from her, at the table. When she stopped speaking, his eyes swept down under the lids and took a narrow peep at her. Their mouths twitched. Suddenly, her loud laugh rang out. He rolled up his handkerchief and stuffed it into his mouth.

The door opened. " What is it ? " asked Roddy.

" Ah, there you see ! " She rocked and sobbed, then stopped and, dabbing her eyes, rose briskly. " The facts of life," she explained.

Roddy, who had also read a pamphlet on how babies are born, was appalled.

" Don't look so hurt ! " she cried. " You are not responsible. You are only a victim."

She stacked up the tray. " You are home very early, Roddy."

" Yes. The Old Man's gone to a conference, so I skipped off. I thought I might be able to give you some help for the party."

" Ah, how kind of you. We'll twist the furniture round in the drawing-room and see what we can make of it." She went out with the tray.

Roddy, who as a leader of men disregarded the intricacies of his own body, looked at Julia's drawing without recognition ; then, conscious that his son now regarded his parents in a new light (and hilariously at that) he murmured " Well, then," rocked on his heels uncertainly for a moment and followed Julia.

Oliver, when his amusement had died down, began to feel he owed his parents some kindness. He was touched that his father had gone to such lengths to bring about his existence and that Julia should have been so bored. ' I must try to be a better son,' he thought. ' I will run wild more and please them.'

Eleanor came in from school and Julia looked round the door from the scullery.

"Oh, haven't you had tea, Eleanor?"

Yes, Eleanor had. With Mr Aldridge, in fact. Chris.

Julia brought in a tray of pastry cases and began to scoop them hollow. "I saw your Mr Aldridge this morning. He was buying himself some collars at Marshalls'. 'Isn't that very wasteful?' I asked him. 'Surely you could manage with what you have for the little time left to you.'"

"Mother!" cried Oliver.

"Don't eat that stuff!" she said, smacking his hand. "It's very indigestible. You'll be awake the whole night. Will your little Mr Aldridge come to-morrow night, Eleanor?"

Eleanor hesitated only for a second or two. "No. I don't think so. But why *my* little Mr Aldridge, and why *little*? Chris is as tall as Roddy, I am quite sure."

"Chris? Chris and Eleanor! Since then we have never looked back."

"You are being very offensive, Julia," said Roddy.

"I know. I think I am tired. I am certainly sick of all this goddam pastry, I should like a drink."

Eleanor slipped upstairs to read the *Daily Worker* where Roddy could not see her. Gradually, the initials were beginning to straighten themselves out.

"Shall we go down to the Grand?" Roddy suggested. "I'll fix the drawing-room while you're getting ready."

"Oh, you are nice to-day!" she cried. "It is just how I feel. I shall never relax *here*. What do you think Eleanor will say?"

"Go and ask her."

"I can stay alone, if she wants to go too," said Oliver. It was his opportunity and quite the least he could do.

"No," said Julia violently. "You ask her, Roddy. She'll do anything for you."

70

"Cowardy custard!"

"Now, Oliver," Julia began briskly. "It is past your bed-time. Run along, do your gargling and remember your teeth, especially the new ones. They have to last you all your life. Try to be a good boy and don't hinder mother. And leave that damn pastry alone."

No, Eleanor didn't mind in the least, said Roddy, and he thought she must be up to mischief in her room, for she didn't ask him in and only opened the door a crack. She was going to bed early, because of the party to-morrow.

"How sensible she is!" said Julia contemptuously. She went upstairs to chivvy Oliver, and to get herself ready. Oliver was in bed already, beginning *Kidnapped* for the second time.

He sat up in his striped pyjamas, with traces of dried tooth-paste round his mouth. Above him was a picture of Mr Lippincote as the Worshipful Master, sitting in the middle of a group of elderly walruses wearing aprons, all looking grave like children in a charade. 'And Mrs had the children to bring up, the servants to intimidate, the meat dishes to cherish and Lady Fennester calling every other day,' Julia thought. 'And then there was shopping at Marshalls', where they would know her and carry her parcels out to the car. And Miss Phyllis would sit kicking her buttoned boots against the counter, watching for the change of more insignificant people, who paid cash, to come shooting back along the overhead wires in a little cage.

'Come, Phyllis, Mamma is ready. Pick up your muff. Good morning, Mr Marshall. Good morning, madam. Good morning, Miss Phyllis.' 'What *I* have seems flimsy and uncertain,' Julia thought. 'I suppose she would never have rushed *her* children into bed so that she might go for a drink. I expect, though,' she comforted herself, 'that the drink would come up with the grocery. And no doubt all the

walruses got deliriously drunk at their orgies and would throw up their aprons and dance.'

" Havers, mon," she said, bending to kiss Oliver.

" Och, gang awa' wi' ye. Have a nice time."

Julia had never set out of an evening without feeling lifted with excitement, her step lighter, her nerves ready for some great event which had never happened, but of which she would not despair for another ten years at least. What it was she hoped for she had not asked herself, yet she did realise dimly that only among other people might she find what she sought, some other person whose words would link together with hers, with whom, she now thought, leaning forward to colour her lips imperfectly, some chord might be struck. She stretched her mouth to the shape of a smile and then laughed at herself in the mirror. ' Those are old roundabout ways of saying it,' she thought, ' words—music. When what I really mean is . . . but no! For that is exactly the last thing I want. *Not* a lover, nor secret notes, not keeping this from Roddy and that from Oliver; ignoring someone in public, to whom in private, in *very* private, I . . . no, it is the last thing.' She stood and shook powder from her skirt.

All the same she could not quell the excitement in her, nor taste without exquisite pleasure the flavour of anticipation. Women die often of an evening, to be renewed again more or less without failure after tea next day. Men merely enjoy themselves.

Roddy was coming up at intervals with pieces of furniture from the drawing-room, little tables and stands for plants, china figures, a lacquered book-trough full of the novels of George Meredith, a Japanese firescreen and a couple of painted fans.

" I am quite ready," Julia announced and came out on to the landing in a white coat with a fine bloom of dirt upon it.

Roddy came up the stairs, carrying a lamp with a fluted

shade and trailing flex. " It looks a different room," he said happily. " Mrs L. would be horrified."

'It certainly has possibilities,' Julia thought, standing in the middle of the rosy room in a suffusion of coppery sunlight. Now almost the whole of the carpet could be seen, velvety and damson-coloured with wreaths of snowy laurel-leaves. She pushed a sofa of striped pink damask against the wall and hid an antique warming pan beneath it.

" Let's go then," said Roddy from the door. " I said goodbye to Eleanor."

" It is nice. I'll have those fans back to-morrow though, I think. How horrid the room smells. Otherwise, lovely."

They shut the door carefully. It was a room they never used. " I hope Mrs L. won't call to-morrow morning," Julia said. " Where did you put all the rubbish?"

" In the maid's room along with the dressmaker's dummy and the fishing rods."

They closed the front door and Julia took her first breath of the brilliant evening air.

.

"My very dear Reggy," Eleanor had written; now she was sitting at the table by her bedroom window, gazing at a little curled cloud drawn up like a boat upon the mackerel sky.

.

In the next room Alan Breck Stewart lay parched on a flat stone in the grilling heat, while the red-coats moved in the bracken all round. Presently, sleep came to him, but the dreams that came with the sleep were the dreams of Oliver Davenant.

.

73

At the Grand, Julia saw Mr Taylor for the first time in his white jacket.

"Damn sure he wears corsets," Roddy murmured.

"Oh, hush!"

"Good evening, madame. Good evening, sir."

Again Julia was shocked to see his face so ruined. When he smiled, gold flashed. He took their order and Julia watched him moving sulkily and sinuously through the little tables towards the bar.

"Why, Rod!" cried Edwards, in sheer astonishment at meeting someone whose company he was scarcely ever without.

Julia felt the atmosphere darkening and saw the Wing Commander standing beside her.

"Good evening, sir," said Roddy, "back already?"

"Back already," his C.O. echoed.

"What are you drinking, sir?" asked Roddy, with false *bonhomie*, trying at the same time to work out which train he could have caught.

"I will take a whisky," said the Wing Commander, sitting down beside Julia. "I have been to a conference," he informed her.

"So I heard," she said encouragingly. Roddy steadily pressed her thigh as he leaned forward, offering cigarettes.

"At Scarborough."

The drinks now arrived, and others were ordered. Mr Taylor withdrew his respect just when, as far as Roddy was concerned, it would have been most acceptable. He merely bowed his head and moved away.

Julia fingered her drink.

"Yes, at Scarborough. Don't wait for me. Drink it up." She took a sip.

"I was thinking of you there," he continued.

"Of me?" She set her glass down in a hurry.

" I spent part of my lunch-hour making a small pilgrimage to Anne Brontë's grave."

" Describe it to me ! "

" The headstone? Oh, a very ugly affair, as you would expect. An unpleasant urn in relief, smothered with some material, draped in rather improbable folds—these local masons, you know—and standing on a couple of books. One large, one small. Well, good luck, Davenant ! And you, my dear ! "

Julia murmured : " One large and one small? What could they mean? "

" Nothing, probably. But then *Agnes Grey* is not a very long book."

" No, indeed. And what else besides the books? "

" Only the name—' Daughter of the Reverend P. Brontë, Incumbent of Haworth, Yorkshire.' And her age—twenty-eight. Railings round about and rough turf. Very windy. Up above, the ruins of a castle and down below, the harbour buildings going down in steps to the sea."

" You make it seem very real."

" I thought of Charlotte standing there, all alone, in the place where I stood—oh, a miserable duty—and then coming back later to fuss because the stone was inscribed wrongly. A woman of great character." He looked at Julia. " Down there, I told myself " (he pointed now at the rich, hotel carpet) " are the very bones. It is difficult to grasp a fact of that nature—that there could be anything tangible left."

" That's true. I suppose bones would be tangible, although one would not, of course, wish to touch them."

He gave her a sharp look and said : " The same again " to Mr Taylor.

" The Old Man buying a drink," Edwards whispered to Roddy, pretending to be blowing his nose.

"You won't be seeing me here again, madame," said Mr Taylor, putting Julia's drink before her and bending towards her confidentially. He wiped the table with a cloth. Roddy blushed. 'Go away,' he willed him silently. But Julia was interested.

"Yes," said Mr Taylor, and his gaze now drew the Wing Commander into the conversation, "as a matter of fact, there's been a bit of nonsense here. . . ."

'His *vile* looks,' Roddy thought, 'corsets, suède shoes, lisp, dyed hair, cockney accent. And Julia's coat dirty, too.'

"So what will you do and where are you going now?" Julia was asking.

"I'm through with working for others," he said proudly. "I only did it to help them out. In the first place. Oh, I shall start on my own, taking over a little club, down by the river. Nothing very elaborate. . . ." He shrugged his shoulders.

"What about . . . ?" The Wing Commander flicked at his glass.

"I think I shall manage."

"Will you write the address down?" Julia asked.

"Oh, Christ!" Roddy groaned to Edwards.

"Certainly, madame."

Julia turned to the Wing Commander. "An odd envelope or something?"

He drew one out of his wallet and handed it to her. Roddy's legs had begun to tremble.

"Wing Commander Mallory," Julia read. "Now a pencil. 'The Kingfisher Club, River Walk.' Oh, that's easy. I could have remembered that."

'*Now* go away,' Roddy willed once more. He wondered if he could possibly have willed it aloud, for Mr Taylor suddenly obeyed him.

"What are we drinking?" Edwards asked loudly.

"We should celebrate, Roddy. It's not often you bring your wife out. Last time I saw you in here was with another woman."

Julia could not restrain herself from looking with quick interest at her husband.

"Oh, it was with his cousin," said Edwards. "Roddy is always fidelity itself, I am sure."

"He had better be," said the Wing Commander, waiting impatiently for another drink.

"What have you been talking about?" Roddy asked his wife in a low, worried voice.

She was trying to free the diamonds of her ring from dried pastry. "About Anne Brontë," she replied. Roddy looked anxious and puzzled.

.

'Your loving E.,' Eleanor wrote. She laid down her pen and, glancing down out of the window, was horrified to see below her in the darkening garden a woman in a white coat gathering roses.

.

"Oh, it must have been Miss Phyllis," said Julia, when Eleanor met them in the hall with her story.

"By the time I got into the garden, she'd gone."

"A damn nerve," Roddy exploded. "It is the last straw. The last straw."

"But she still can't rid herself of the feeling that it's her house. That's understandable."

"I don't see it."

"But you yourself gave her mother permission to come and go to that room."

"*With* permission. And nothing was said about picking flowers in the garden at all hours."

"At all hours! This is the first time."

"How do you know?"

"I am not a nervous woman," Eleanor was beginning, so Julia went upstairs. Roddy followed, and Eleanor followed him, doggedly, reasonably explaining.

Julia went into Oliver's room. He lay with his face against the pillow, peaceful, flushed and beautiful. She wished all the world might see him like this. He awoke drowsily as she took the book from under his shoulder. "I was dreaming I was killing you," he murmured.

She closed the door and found Eleanor still explaining on the landing. "I don't believe in all that nonsense about Freud," said Julia. "Dreams just happen—any old nonsense comes out of the tangle. It doesn't *mean* anything."

It broke into Eleanor's repetitions and they moved towards their bedrooms, saying 'good-night'.

CHAPTER 9

JULIA HAD one beautiful frock. It was made of striped bolster ticking, black and white, and in its stiff folds she looked like Mrs Siddons. Standing at the mirror with the rose-pink room behind her, she was pleased with herself. But not with the room, she decided, turning round. It waited. Chairs and sofa held out empty arms imploringly. Roses stood at attention. Ashtrays were disposed too carefully. Mrs Lippincote, in her court feathers and long gloves, surveyed them very disdainfully from the bureau. Julia popped her in a drawer.

Roddy, coming in, couldn't see that it was all wrong. He

78

stood there with two aspirins in the palm of one hand and a glass of water in the other. He wished all the guests would arrive at once, bursting in with exuberance, and in no time at all become semi-intoxicated. As a host, he liked things easy.

Julia had more courage. The aspirins shocked her. She took them from him and dropped them into a rose-bowl, together with the water. "Never let guests feel they have come at the beginning," she said. "It's true someone *must* be first, but *we* are here. So bring some drinks and let's begin." She took an armful of cushions and threw them from a distance into the chairs, and then pulled one of the roses to pieces and scattered the petals. Roddy ladled out a concoction which was mainly poor Burgundy and bits of cucumber and which the women were expected to drink.

Eleanor came in, wearing a black frock and what is often described as 'amusing' jewellery. "Have you begun already?" she said disapprovingly, seeing the glass in Julia's hand. "Oliver wants some wine."

"Oh, Roddy, take this drop to him and fill the glass with warm water."

Roddy was horrified.

"But, of course, you can," Julia cried impatiently. "Young girls used always to drink it at bedtime. Look at Catherine Morland!"

"I never knew her," said Roddy, filling a plate for Oliver with little sandwiches and asparagus rolled in thin bread and margarine.

"Not too many of those," Julia warned him.

A knock at the door galvanised all three of them. Eleanor shot upstairs with the wine-glass, and Roddy summoned all his geniality and went to open the door. The Wing Commander might have known better than to arrive first. His wife, plump and black-satined, like a seal with a rope of

pearls round its neck, was led chattering to a corner, where a glass was put into her hand, over which she exclaimed in a grateful way, as if it were the last thing she had allowed herself to expect.

"And are you getting on any better with Mr B.?" she asked Julia, referring to the butcher. "I was glad I chanced to meet you there the other day. When I saw him giving you that piece of skirt I was flabbergasted. I simply didn't know what to say or think. But what could I have done? I couldn't make a scene in the shop, but the minute you'd gone, I leant over the counter and said very quietly: 'That lady happened to come here on my recommendation and I was very much shocked when I saw what you gave her just now.' That long grain and the way the gristle ran—I don't like to see it in beef and I told him so. I'm glad he had the grace to colour up."

Eleanor was introduced. "How d'you do!" said Mrs Mallory. "And I hope you're getting your liver all right. That wants watching, too. I wouldn't put it past him to slip in a piece of pigs' liver from time to time; in fact, I suffered myself from that when Harry was first posted here. Until I made it quite clear. He's—no, not unscrupulous—I won't say that. But . . . *sharp*. I suppose one has to be in trade nowadays, and I will put up with a great deal from him because of his mutton. To-day, for instance, we had a little piece of neck with some new carrots and parsley, just one little onion and pearl barley. And it simply slipped off the bones. Slipped off. No, he just wants watching. Ah, here comes the Adjutant!"

"You must excuse me," said Julia, leaving her to Eleanor. "I've not yet met the Fieldings."

Mrs Mallory turned to Eleanor. "They are Regular Air Force, dear, but very nice people," she explained.

.

Upstairs, Alan Breck Stewart, sturdy, short, pocked-marked, lay in Cluny's cage, playing Carte and drinking whisky. The wine became fainter each time Oliver refilled the glass, until now it was the merest blush in the water. Every time the gate banged, he stopped being Breck Stewart and hopped out of bed to look severely upon the arriving guests.

.

"Well!" said the Wing Commander. He picked up a fold of Julia's skirt and fingered it. "I should like to paint you in this pink room, with all the glasses and roses and wearing this fine frock."

"Oh, can you paint, then?"

He finished his glass. "No," he said mournfully, folding his arms across his chest.

"Let me get you another drink," she suggested.

"No. Stay where you are."

"Roddy will be cross with me if you have nothing to drink."

"We can both deal with Roddy's crossness, I think. Let me see you sitting on this sofa. Tell me, are you quite happy here?"

"No, of course not. One is never quite happy anywhere. Or never more than just on and off."

"Just on and off," he repeated. "I see. Are you laughing at me all the time?"

She looked up quickly and he was surprised at the candour of her expression. "No."

"Just on and off?" he persisted.

"Only when you are being Mr Rochester, or more than usually dour."

"You find me dour, then?"

"Yes, very. I can't imagine what look your face would have if you were to laugh, smile even."

81

" I see." He was still looking gravely at her.

" You pursue your gloom as if it were a vocation. Let me fetch you a drink now."

" Please, no! I shall not stay very long, so let us talk for a while."

" What was your job before you joined up?" she asked him kindly.

" I shall not tell you," he replied. " It is what they all want to find out and I cannot have junior officers discussing me in that way."

" But if you make a mystery of it they will think it something shameful or ridiculous—a *procureur* or a bookie." She laughed with delight at the idea.

" They will have thought of those already. You think I have an exaggerated idea of my position? Is that so?"

She nodded, feeling it difficult to tell lies to this man.

" And you find it painful to talk to me, moreover."

" Oh, no! Never that. Not to anyone."

" This is a pleasant party," he said, his glance travelling round the room and taking in his wife, who was talking to Mrs Fielding now. " Chilprufe from Marshalls," he heard her saying. And then something about Felicity and ' highly strung '. He sighed.

" You sigh over my pleasant party, even," said Julia gently.

" You are right," he said, returning to her. " I have not the capacity for enjoyment. You will say it is because I am always bothering myself and those around me with my own importance, my dignity. You would be wrong. You could not be expected to be right."

" I find it difficult to understand you, that's true enough."

" And I you! Well, that is an excellent basis for friendship. All that any of us wants is to be misunderstood. Those who put it the other way round are hypocrites." As he said

the word, he looked up at Roddy, who came towards them.

"But you have nothing to drink," Roddy exclaimed. "Julia, how could you!"

He was wishing the C.O. would go home. It was high time, and Edwards and some of the others were getting a little noisy and over-confident. Mrs Fielding had a glazed and stricken look as she sat fascinated by Mrs Mallory, listening, counting the pearls, failing, listening, losing grip . . . Roddy's own head was endeavouring to float away from his shoulders.

"We are not interested in drinking," said the Wing Commander, with magnificent egotism. Julia twirled her empty glass in her lap. "We were having a private conversation." But Roddy had not the wit to go away. It never occurred to him that he was anything but welcome wherever he went.

"I was trying to discover something," said the Wing Commander, not because he had relented towards Roddy, but because he could say in a tortuous way what he could not say directly. "I find your wife a mysterious woman. I was hoping to discover the secret, some clue." He looked at Julia as he spoke.

"We do not try to find out Julia's secrets," Roddy said distinctly. "She tries to find out ours."

For the first time the Wing Commander saw her moved and put out. Her hands trembled in her lap and tightened against the stem of the glass, a red stain appeared on her cheek as if Roddy had struck her. To ease the anger of her silence, Mallory stooped to pleasantry. "Oh come, my dear, tell me what you think is my secret vice."

"Opium for sure," she managed to say lightly. She let him lead her gently from one anecdote to another, and so on, until the moment of anger was a pinpoint in the distance.

Roddy, unperturbed, and wondering how De Quincey

and Branwell Brontë had come into the conversation, brought drinks for them and drifted away. His heart was at home with Edwards and his crowd, but the Wing Commander's presence unsettled him; as soon as he began to enjoy himself, he would begin also to wonder what brick Julia was now dropping, and how he might contrive to move her away and put Mrs Fielding in her place.

"We shall go now," the Wing Commander was saying. "It has been lovely, and you have been lovely too." Julia stood up and smoothed her dress. She watched him cross the room to summon his wife, watched her being drawn reluctantly away from Mrs Fielding, heard the feverish repetitions, admonitions, of Chilprufe, Marshalls, nonshrink and double reinforcement.

"My dear," said Mrs Mallory, coming now to pause beside Julia. "What a nice party! What lovely things you've given us to eat! Now, have I got everything, Robert? Gloves and handbag? And thank you very much, Mr Davenant. I hope you will come to us. . . . Really delightful. Ah, Robert! What will Mrs Davenant think of you!" For he had lifted Julia's fingers and kissed them.

"If ever there's anything you want," he murmured, as they reached the front door.

"Good-night, sir! Very sorry you have to go so soon," said Roddy, speaking loudly and forthrightly and in competition with the sudden increase of noise from within. When the door had shut, "Good" he said, rubbing his hands together, and made quickly for the drawing-room, where Edwards had Mrs Lippincote's carpet in jeopardy, with a beer mug on his head and a wild look in his eyes.

At about two o'clock they were left alone to clear up. "It was a good party," said Eleanor, yawning, and emptying ash-trays into the grate, and knowing the evening had not satisfied her nor delighted her as once it would have done.

"A damn good party," Roddy agreed. "It *was* good, Julia, wasn't it?" He cast himself down on the sofa with a bunch of cheese straws in his hand.

"Yes," she said gravely. She took up some empty bottles and went out. She had been angry with him on many occasions, impatient often, never grave.

CHAPTER 10

ON HOT summer afternoons in Vasco Street, Sarge would take tea out into the yard and sit under the great vine, waiting for Vera. It was an ancient vine and had its roots there at the back of the shop, but its twisting branches covered the walls of several houses. After a hot summer it would bear bunches of small tough-skinned but sweet grapes, then its leaves would come down in a great clutter over the little bits of garden and fill gutterings and choke drains. Sarge liked to sit there making notes for lectures and articles, in his slow schoolboyish writing, until Vera came home, laying her cool hands over his eyes, drawing his head back against her breast. He would take her hands and bring them down to his mouth. Then someone would come. It was like this all the time. Their love was kept at an uncertain level by the presence of others, by those, moreover, whom they loved and chose to live and work with. This love was never allowed to supersede or interfere with the work from which it had grown. Work stood between them, as the world stands between the betrothed, and a true knowledge of what their love might ultimately be was something they had not yet achieved.

When he was working on the night shift, he had always

this peaceful time to himself, when the house was empty and the clock, which they both thought so beautiful, ticked loudly in the front room. He would wake up in the untidy sunlit bedroom; but there is a staleness and feeling of lassitude about waking in the afternoon. Long after he was up, he would still be drowsy and have the taste of sleep in his mouth. He would pad from room to room in his stockinged feet, calmed by the peace and emptiness, and then he would settle down with his letters and pamphlets and wait for Vera to come home first. Sometimes she didn't. Sometimes she was the second or third to come, but it was all right, because then to-morrow she might succeed. He could picture her bicycling to him through the town, holding her skirt down over one bare knee, her brown, rather shiny legs pedalling furiously, her black hair whipped back from her shoulders, the books bouncing in the basket.

Leo, who did most of the cooking, was neat and orderly so that the kitchen, unless the girls had been there, was as tidy as the laboratory where he worked all day, and Sarge made as little mess as possible while he was getting tea. The kitchen was downstairs behind the shop. It was dark and filled with a green submarine light, for its one window was thickly fringed with vine leaves. The brick floor was often silvered by slugs, and fantastic spiders would be found sitting crookedly in the sink. The yard outside was full of crates from the grocer's shop and tongue-ferns grew between the cobblestones.

The grocer had been a Socialist all his life, and his chief pleasure now was for Sarge to come in at tea-time and sit on the empty biscuit tins, chewing a handful of currants, and asking his advice. The young people upstairs were wonderful to him and he would have joined the Communist Party now, at his age ("What, at my age?" he would chuckle, measuring out sago into blue bags) but that he

feared Sarge would then stop arguing with him. "My young people upstairs," he would boast at his daughter-in-law's, where he lived now his wife was dead. "Of course they walk in and out of the shop when they like. They've got their keys, and how else are they to come and go?" Then he would wait for the inevitable expression of doubt, so that he could add proudly: "We are not landlord and tenants. We are Communists and trust one another."

People were always coming and going up the stairs. He came to know most of them; Chris, for instance, and then Eleanor. It was different from his daughter-in-law's, where people only came to tea on Sundays and dinner must be early because of it and scones made first and tempers lost. He would always remember the early days when Vera came into the shop and said at once in her direct way: "We shall not be buying our groceries from you, Mr Speed. It wouldn't be right for us not to deal with the Co-op." She had looked at him and waited. Had the others sent her to explain, he wondered. He decided not, for there was something unpremeditated in her actions, which gave the impression that, as soon as her mind was made up, she moved.

He took his glasses off and polished them and looked up at his row of old-fashioned pink canisters with their gilt lettering. "My dear," he said, "I would never choose this life if I were starting again, although I've been happy and it has lasted me out. But it will never last another generation out. Part of the old loneliness." He pointed with his spectacles at the shelf of canisters. "There's pride in it, but then there usually is in loneliness. When you're not lonely, when you have a lot of people, then you don't need to find *things* to take a pride in. So it's time we came out of our little shops and took part in life itself. But *not* at *my* age."

She smiled. "Are there really the right things in those

jars? Or is it like ours, which is marked RICE and is full of clothes pegs?"

He lifted down a jar marked DRIED FRUIT, wiped the lid and raised it, and tipped towards her the large clear golden raisins. "Give me your hand then." He took it and filled it with raisins, and when he had put the jar back on the shelf, he said: "So you won't come shopping with me. It's to be the Co-op, is it? Well! Mind the seeds in those."

"And so you forgive us?" she said.

But he shook his head. "If you are right, you don't need to be forgiven."

Vera went back upstairs to make out the shopping list with Kirsty. "There is never to be any running downstairs for a tin of sardines or a blue-bag," she said sternly. "Anything we've forgotten, we must go without. We are not just to have principles while we remember, and make a convenience of him when we forget."

"Heaven knows what we'd be doing with a blue-bag," said Kirsty.

.

It was a sultry afternoon, a bit thundery. Sarge had roused himself, shaved, folded Vera's pyjamas and his own and made his bed. He took up his books and went down-stairs. On his way to the kitchen, he looked into the shop but Mr Speed was doing up his weekly orders. The shop door-bell pinged and Eleanor came in. It was the first time she had been here alone, but Chris was at the Grammar School and coming later.

"Why, hallo, Eleanor!" said Sarge. They went out into the kitchen together. It was infinitely pleasing to her to have someone say 'Why, hallo, Eleanor' in just the way he did.

"We'll have tea outside, shall we? Where could Leo have put the milk bottle?" It was under the sink in a bowl of

water and draped with wet muslin. "Very methodical, Leo," he remarked, pouring the milk into the jug with a great rush.

"How did Leo . . .?" Eleanor began.

Sarge turned round, the jug in his hand. "In Germany," he said. "He was all right till he got out and then it happened: nervous reaction, some muscular thing, I suppose."

"When was that?"

"Before the war."

"And will it come back, d'you think?"

He grimaced.

"Doesn't look much like it, does it?"

"No." She watched him getting the tray ready for tea, counting saucers, unhooking cups from the dresser. "No, it doesn't." She thought: men love one another in a way one has to respect.

They left the tray ready on the table until Vera should come and went out to the little patch of worn grass under the leafy wall.

"There was a dreadful party last night," she said rather falsely. "My head has banged and hammered all day. Roddy measures the success of a party by how many people feel ill the following day." She lit a cigarette. Sarge didn't smoke. He didn't drink either, but he said: "Does you good to have a bit of a beer-up now and then."

Eleanor fingered her forehead ruefully. "Oh, I don't *know*. All through the party itself I am saying *stupid* things. In the morning I wake up and my ears are full of my own voice going yap, yap, yap, and I remember—some people forget, but they're lucky. I can't—I just remember everything I've said and feel ashamed. Then I can't *bear* my breakfast and my head thunders. All day, when the children are not driving me mad, I am trying to persuade myself that no one else will be in a condition to remember what I've said.

But I never quite convince myself enough to stop feeling ashamed."

"It doesn't sound much good. Does Roddy go in for these things a lot?"

"It's Julia. Parties excite her. Drink excites her. But even Julia seemed subdued to-day."

Sarge had little imagination. He couldn't picture that world at all. "Are you coming to the meeting to-night?" he asked, fingering his notebook.

"I don't know." She tugged up the fine dry grass and scattered it. She frowned.

"Is it your job?" he asked. "Same as Chris?"

"No, I don't quite see it like Chris about the job. No, it's Roddy."

Sarge knew when to wait and when to speak. Now he leant back and waited, and hoped it would not be for too long.

"Oh, I know he's not my husband," said Eleanor suddenly, as if she were speaking his thoughts for him, which was not true, as he was thinking of Vera.

"But you have to live there?" he suggested.

"No, it's not even that. I don't have to live there. I can't think how I do sometimes. No, I can please myself where I live, although they were kind to me when I was ill."

"Would Roddy object so much, if you . . ."

"Furious! Oh, he'd be furious. And hurt. And so ashamed. People like—like *you* are beyond the pale. He despises you and is afraid. It worries me so much. I lie and think of it in the night."

"What does Chris say?" Sarge asked, trying to shift the burden.

"Oh, Chris has other things on his mind."

"He has, has he?" Sarge smiled broadly. "You're very fond of your cousin? Is that it?"

She looked up gratefully, her eyes almost full. "Yes, I . . . yes. I think my life would break in two, if I were to break away from him."

"Well, it's up to you," he said vaguely. "If you can't have both, you must invent a situation where you'd have to choose, and make up your mind *now* which you'd do without. I can't help you. I can only say that no good seems to come from ruining your personal life. I've seen too much of it."

"You've seen too much of what?" asked Vera, coming out with the tray. "Hallo, Eleanor. Where's Chris?"

"He's coming later." She wished they wouldn't always link her with Chris, that they would sometimes let her be on her own.

"Kirsty's just coming. She's washing her feet because they ache. And here's Leo!" Vera began to pour out tea.

"Eleanor no sugar. Leo no milk. Kirsty two spoonfuls. Vera no sugar. And here's the basin, Sarge, for you." He spooned sugar in until Eleanor shuddered, then he began to stir and stir and stir. Leo sat on the grass, shut away in his private world. "Leo, you'll get your pain in your leg again," said Vera. "Fetch one of Mr. Speed's boxes to sit on." He smiled and shook his head, drawing a blade of grass between his teeth.

Kirsty came out and flopped down. "It's going to thunder," she said. "I feel it in my head."

"And I, too," Eleanor smiled.

"And the air has a different quality," said Vera. "Voices carry so oddly."

Leo looked up. A large indigo cloud, the shape of the Cherbourg Peninsula, towered above them, and certainly the trees were sharply green against the mulberry sky, and strangely lucid.

"What time are we going?" asked Vera.

91

'We!' thought Eleanor. Excitement trembled through her. 'But I *must* be part of that. I have so seldom been *part* of anything. Isn't it my one chance to be what I want to be?'

"We shall get wet," she said aloud. Sarge looked at her curiously and smiled and nodded. She breathed the thin cooling air in sips, felt with exquisite joy the grass pressing against her palm, leaving red criss-crosses on the side of her leg.

"Look!" cried Vera. She had been exploring the vine leaves. "There are the baby grapes! Little bunches." She went up on tiptoe and they could see, from where they sat, the little green bunch with its fine tendrils against the pink of her hand. "Oh, the hundreds of tiny bunches. It's smothered with them."

"It's going to be a vintage year," said Sarge.

"Oh, Sarge! We'll make wine. We'll have one of those weeks, a fiesta, a wine-pressing week. We won't go to work. We'll just stand about in the sun and squash the grapes through our toes."

"Does one wash one's feet for that?" asked Eleanor.

"Oh, only for the *white* wine," Kirsty giggled.

A large spot of rain, the size of a shilling, fell on the cobbles. Vera stood up among the leaves, suddenly stilled, sleepily warm in the heat from the brick wall.

Sarge looked at the rain spot, then at Eleanor. "We'll lend you a mac," he said.

"And here is Chris at last!" cried Kirsty.

CHAPTER 11

"RODDY, I WANT to go out this evening." He had just settled in his chair after supper. The rain had come to nothing and now the sun had come through again.

"It isn't like you to ask permission." He smiled indulgently. "Where shall we go? Eleanor seems to be out, though."

"I mean I want to go alone."

"I will not even ask where," he said grandly, and waited. She said nothing. "But don't go into pubs on your own," he began to stipulate.

"I am not going *in* anywhere. I am going for a walk." She looked out of the window, wondering why she submitted to him, standing there like a child waiting for him to pat her head and give her sixpence. He thought she was tired after the party.

"It must be just one hell of a hang-over to force you out on a walk."

Upstairs, she sat on the edge of the bed in her grubby white coat and wondered where she could go. To whom? She sat there until after she had heard Roddy go out into the garden. She could hear the irregular clip-clip of the shears as he trimmed the privet and, when she roused herself at last to look out, could see the sprinkler spinning water over the lettuces, a mist of water with a little rainbow.

She put a pound note in her cigarette case and a few coppers loose in her pocket and went quickly out of the house and along the Crescent. She waited under the lime tree at the corner for a bus. In a panic, she watched the couples sauntering; young people, lovers. 'I am quite alone,' she thought. 'In that house there are Roddy and Eleanor

93

ranged against me, facing me from a great distance, like cliffs one sees from a long way off, with no birds flying or flags waving, or windows glinting, not a sign of recognition at all.' She got on a bus headed for the prison. 'And Oliver?' she went on to herself, holding up her coppers and taking the ticket, 'but it is wrong to make use of a child. I have done it too much already, may God forgive me!'

Along the pavements straggled little boys with fishing-nets and handkerchiefs knotted on their heads, their trousers rolled up still from their paddling, and jam-jars—in which there were weeds at least, if not minnows—swinging on loops of string. She thought of the river and the prison and then of the Abbey ruins, imagining a dark, Gothic, ivy-covered place in which, under some crumbling archway, she might meet the Wing Commander, with the bats swinging at shoulder-height and a white owl hooting above. 'And if life were only a novel by Charlotte Brontë,' she thought, stepping down from the bus, 'I *should* meet him there. It would be the fit and proper thing to do.'

She found herself in a mean street leading to the river. Doors with white china knobs opened on to the pavement. At some of them, old women sat on chairs, hands spread on aprons, with a vision over their shoulders of painted ornaments standing on silk table runners. Up the street came the little boys with their nets, youths with open shirts and segments of sunburn on their chests, tired mothers with baskets, little girls with bunches of reeds, all going wearily home. There was the prison, with its red and yellow patterned brickwork and its dagger-like windows, and the river itself beginning to be felt, a sense of space and the scent of it on the air. A pub door stood open and the coolness from within, the smell of the wet trampled sawdust and the beer, hung over the pavement. She hesitated, but in her mind only, and then walked on. On the bridge she leant against the parapet

94

and looked down at the moving river dinted with light. An absurd little puff of sound came from a steamer, which slid towards the bridge, canopied, Victorian, fussy, casting out a great fan-shaped wake which slapped against the stone piers and the sandbags along one bank and swished into the rushes on the other. Beyond the few buildings, one or two riverside bungalows and the moored house-boats, lay the wide water meadows and the river moving down through them in the sunset, and at the other side of the bridge a mass of high ruins and children playing hide-and-seek among them.

She crossed the bridge and went along the gravelled walks, through immense lawn-floored rooms open to the sky, with pink flowers growing in tufts twenty feet high on the flinty stone. Children ran up the twisting steps of the Abbot's stairs. They led nowhere, they ended in the sky, these steps, and the children dared not jump from so high ; they screamed with pleasure and ran down again. Julia sat on a seat to watch them. She lit a cigarette and leaned back, feeling curiously at peace, idle, independent. ' I am doing something for myself alone, that's the reason,' she thought. ' No one else has the tiniest part in it.'

But she was wrong, for there, sauntering along under the walls was, not the Wing Commander as it should have been, but Mr Taylor. He saw her, the gold flashed in his smile but his eyes could not follow suit, they were the dull eyes of a very ill or of a haunted person.

' Oh, I don't want to be " madamed " this evening,' she thought crossly, patting the seat beside her in a welcoming way. But she was to be merely Mrs Davenant, it appeared.

" It's an old-fashioned place," he said, surveying the massive Norman walls. " I usually take a stroll round of an evening. Get a breath of fresh air."

" But what about your club? "

" That's what I mean. Gets so stuffy in there. I feel I've

got to get out for ten minutes. Greta can manage on her own. My secretary," he added with simple modesty.

'I wonder,' thought Julia, 'where *she* has sprung from?'

"Truth is," he continued, "that atmosphere's no good for me. Something wrong with the old ticker." He touched his heart with his gold-ringed hand. "Stopped me from getting in the Army. I had the offer of a commission in the H.A.C., but I couldn't take it up."

"Is your club near here?" Julia asked, when she had finished murmuring sympathy.

"Why, yes, just along the bank. Originally, it was my sister's week-end place. She's an actress, but she doesn't get down much now, what with the war."

'Those children ought to be in bed,' Julia thought. 'Yet they all look far healthier than Oliver.'

"And how is your club doing?"

"Oh, fair enough, you know. Would you care to take a stroll along with me? It would give me very much pleasure if you could spare time to come in for a drink."

'A drink!' she thought. The desire to see Greta was also more than she could manage to resist. They left the seat and walked down a rocky avenue marked 'Cloister'. 'This is an adventure in a way,' she told herself. 'As much as ever a married woman and a mother can hope for.'

"Now this!" she said, stopping before a shallow stone trough with a railing, "is it a grave, or a fireplace or what?"

"I couldn't say," said Mr Taylor, who thought it was a urinal; but wild horses, as they say, could not have drawn such an opinion from him.

Dormitory and Refectory they passed through and that was all. Julia looked back at the greenish sky through an arch and also above it, and the panic of tears gathered in her. Yet she would look. Surprisingly, suddenly, the children's voices had gone. It is a thing that happens on summer

96

nights; one moment they are all there and then without a call or a warning they are gone, but it is difficult to be sure whether they go because they sense the mystery of oncoming night, or whether the oncoming night is mysterious because they are gone. The silence in the ruins, at any rate, was ominous, discounting the centuries, reminding one of the swift passage of time and of mortality.

"Rather eerie at night," said Mr Taylor.

"Yes, indeed." Julia cast a last look backwards.

"A bit different from Soho. Though half Soho's in ruins now."

"But not quite the same ruins," she observed, thinking of the planks lying across rubble, the dust, the faded wallpaper and pink willowstrife growing among the masonry. He was thinking of it, too, with love and emotion. On those pavements, he had been known and recognised. He had loved the morning outings with Louise, watching her quick fingers among endive and artichokes; liked to see her buying a pear or melon or choosing asparagus; following her into the cool shops for spaghetti, garlic, boxes of sardines, or thin batons of bread. 'Bombed out' is a phrase the world was now used to. "But you were lucky," people would say, "not to have been sleeping there." "No, no one was hurt," he would say. It was like a game of tennis, that sort of conversation: the ball went back and forth but no one was really involved, the expected replies were dealt and after the game had been kept up for a while, the other side tired and, feeling it had done well, changed the subject. But the truth had not been spoken. Had he suddenly said: "My life ended just the same, whether I was killed or not. This that I have now means nothing to me and has no value," they would still not have understood.

They were walking along by the river now. It wore a polished look under the darkening sky.

"One day on my birthday," said Julia suddenly, "you had prepared a special lunch, although the war was on then. Jellied *consommé*—oh, how I love summer food!—salmon and a green mayonnaise, a lovely pale smooth green, and strawberries. And then you sent us over some kümmel. As a present. I've never forgotten one mouthful or sip of that meal. You see, I like a great hue and cry on my birthday. And you had laid a rose beside my plate."

"It must be your birthday soon," he said, thinking of the strawberries.

"Yes." She was politely reticent, as if she would say no more lest he should feel himself forced to buy her a present. "The kümmel, that was kind of you."

"My kümmel!" he sighed. 'My stock!' he would think in the middle of the night, seeing the different bottles—the slim, the round, all the shapes and colours of them, the bottles with the gilt and greenish labels with beautifully printed chateaux and the fine names, the stone bottles of Cusenier, the red seals, the little chains round their necks, the Chianti in their gay baskets. But it could never be grieved-over in public, because human beings had been lost, and this was only wine. Now life was measuring out gin and Italians to tarts and bottled beers to officers. All women who went out with officers he thought tarts. Even in Soho, he had not liked officers, for he thought they showed off over wine-lists while their womenfolk giggled and said they 'didn't mind,' or 'anything would be nice' and 'leave it to you.' He had often decided that he would rather have the greedy elderly women, mixing their own salads with their ringed fingers, eating in silence. Most of all, he had loved Julia, for she had eaten in his restaurant as if she were a guest.

"Here we are!" he now said jauntily, holding open the gate of a rickety little bungalow. Dance music trailed dismally over the lawn. He took Julia's elbow as they entered

98

a dusty hall, cheaply smart with silver paint and balloon fabric, and led her into the room where a few people shuffled on a square of linoleum, going wretchedly round and round like convicts taking exercise, and a few more sat on high stools at the bar, shouting. Dancers and drinkers alike looked at Julia with contempt, but Julia was looking round for Greta.

She was too busy, as a rule, measuring up and deploring other people to be in any way conscious of herself. This evening, for instance, Mr Taylor was to be set against his background and Greta's importance there assessed, her role decided upon. There would be raw material enough to weave dreams, for many an hour washing up, ironing or shelling peas, those times when the body divides, one part set down firmly before the sink, but the mind all the time tacking, veering, going forward at a fair pace in no particular direction, not quite so much like Emily Brontë learning German grammar while she kneaded bread as Julia liked to suppose.

" Miss Warburton. Mrs Davenant."

" How d'you do " and " How d'you do." So little beneath the smiles of both lay disguised the swift calculation, the summing-up. Their eyes, so socially bright, seemed not to travel from the face of the other, but somehow the dirty white coat, the expensive ring, the blown hair of the one, and the chipped nail varnish, the charm-bracelet and elaborate coiffure of the other, were noted without the smallest hesitation. To shake hands, Miss Warburton had leant over the bar, across the tops of glasses. She did so as if she were offering herself up ; her breasts hung in her dress like little unripe pears.

' She frightens me,' Julia thought tranquilly.

Miss Warburton now polished tumblers and over her shoulder returned the badinage of two Australian officers.

The brittle back-chat flew back and forth like splintering glass.

Mr Taylor wanted Julia to have 'something nice', but she would have only beer. "There is some good brandy," he said in a low voice.

"No. Only beer."

Miss Warburton swept a cloth in damp scallops along the bar.

"A beer?"

"Me, too, Greta, please."

'Was her glance at him one of contempt?' Julia could not help wondering.

He took the two glasses of beer and led the way to a divan in the corner. The orange cover had been kicked up, revealing the grubby pink blankets underneath.

Whose bed was it? Julia wondered, sitting down reluctantly. Whoever slept there must be doomed to a fine haze of smoke in the morning, and the reminder of last night's beer.

"I wish you would have had the brandy," he murmured.

"No. Another time." She took a long drink at the beer. Each time she looked at him she was shocked anew. "I think you're ill," she said.

"Yes, I'm ill all right. Get some very nasty turns now and then. I don't think this atmosphere's much good for heart trouble."

Atmosphere's one word for it, Julia conceded. Aloud she asked: "Do you sleep in here?" She had often had success with this method of attack; outrageous questions had been answered by shocking people into an unpremeditated reply. Mr Taylor, however, was listless. He merely nodded, his eyes 'pleins de chagrin', as she had once written in an essay at school on 'Le Singe'. "And I don't suppose the blitzes did it any good either," he added. "Those terrible nights.

You get up in the morning with your stomach tender from the fear you've been in all night. Can't be any good for you, can it?" Put in this way, air-raids became a matter like taking snuff or smoking; to be indulged in or given up as one might think wise. "And then," he continued, "there are all the people who refuse to have their morale destroyed. They're the worst part of the whole affair. Sometimes you feel it would be such a relief to say you're frightened, but those awful people stop you. You go about all day longing to tell someone you've lost your nerve, or to hear someone say the same thing to you, but it never happens."

"But you are telling someone now," Julia reminded him.

"Oh, now, it doesn't matter. Not since that morning when I saw the Charlotte razed to the ground—whatever that may mean."

He went to fetch more beer from the bar. Miss Warburton murmured something without looking at him as she flopped the beer into the glasses. Julia heard him say "Oh, for Christ's sake!" as he turned away. 'Perhaps *I* am making trouble,' she thought placidly. Roddy now seemed a long way from her. To walk out of the house alone, to be where they could not find her, was like sloughing off an old skin. The gesture itself had refreshed her. The gesture in itself was something. 'And perhaps even Nora Helmer returned the next day,' she thought, taking her beer from Mr Taylor.

"I suppose," she said (for this was an opportunity), "that only the very tail-end of bottles goes into dishes like your *Turbot au vin blanc*?" He sipped his beer. "Or perhaps none at all?" she added bravely. "It doesn't matter. It's only that one likes to know, that one hopes not to be fooled."

When he had sipped quietly a little longer, he said, as if he were quoting the words: "The English cook is a terrible combination of wastefulness and meanness. She would

throw into the dustbin what a French family would make
a meal from . . ."

"Yes, we know all that," said Julia impatiently. "Perso-
nally, I think they're welcome. I loathe that French family
gathered round the dustbin and having a high old feast from
potato peelings and fish-bones decorated with carrot tops."

"But," he continued, and she had nearly made him
swerve from his course, "mention a teaspoonful of brandy
to brighten up their dreary food and they throw up their
hands in horror."

"It is a French gesture, throwing up the hands, not
English," Julia objected. "I should have liked to have seen
into your kitchen."

"Women often say that." He was thinking of the muddle
down there, the chef wiping a finger across his spoon and
then into his mouth to taste, the spirals of apple-peelings
under the hard electric light, the awful rows going on.
"Cooking is not a woman's job."

"Oh, God!" she laughed. "If only we had never to do
the jobs which are not ours!"

"Your laughter does me good."

Suddenly, she thought: 'He is truly ill. He has the mind
of a sick or very old person—sincerely occupied with what is
or is not good for him. When we are young, or well, we say
"I like" or "I hate"; we never say "It is good for me,"
"It is bad for me."'

Finishing her beer, she said: "I must go."

"Before you go, will you promise to come again?" He
spoke with the urgency of a child.

"Yes. I will promise that."

"I'll ring for a taxi, then."

"Oh, no!" She laid a hand on his arm as he moved. "I
want to walk. I came out to walk and I'm determined
to."

"But not at this time of night," he protested. "Not on your own."

"At my age," she assured him, "it is quite safe."

"Oh, no!" He blushed. "Then I shall come with you." This made her laugh again, so that one of the officers shuffling by said: "Now, Charles!" in a mocking voice.

"Walk back past the ruins with me then. At the bridge I'm all right."

She bade Miss Warburton good-night, noting with pleasure a little wing of grey above each temple. Outside, a Gothic mist rose from the river and wreathed about the ruins.

"You get on all right with your secretary?" she asked.

"Oh, she's very efficient. Sometimes, she's difficult. The situation is really a bit complicated, for I allowed her to put a little money into this concern. Not altogether wise, I suppose." He shrugged.

"Any owls in these ruins?"

"Never seen any. Never heard any, either, not any noise like I imagined owls making. 'To-whit, to-whoo', and all that. What will your husband say, you being out so late on your own?" It was his turn to be inquisitive.

"He's my husband. Not my keeper," said Julia crossly, and in some ways not quite truthfully, for she knew that Roddy would be waiting up to expostulate.

"Are you a suffragette?"

"My mother was," she said with asperity.

They reached the bridge and leaned for a moment on the parapet. The river slid under the arches, dividing silkily at the piers, empty, free of the scum of little boats, unruffled by oars. When she straightened her back to go, he took her hand.

"I would never have dared to hope for such an evening as this has been." His eyes were consistently mournful. "You

bring back the old days for me, and the best part of the old days."

As she walked by herself over the bridge, she thought: 'I am never worthy of the way people talk to me,' and the tears pricked her eyes.

．　　　．　　　．　　　．　　　．

When the door opened, Roddy threw down his newspaper. But it was Eleanor returning from her meeting. She glanced at the clock as she looked in on her way to bed. "I'm late," she said gaily, "I spent the evening with Threlly and Cowper. Time goes quickly gossiping." As she went upstairs, she was astonished at the ease with which the lies had been spoken.

And presently the door opened again, and Roddy threw down his paper once more. This time, of course, it was Julia. She brought in a smell of the open air, but also a perceptible smell of beer, standing there by the door, untying her belt.

"I was getting anxious," he began.

"Oh, nothing ever happens to *me*," she said lightly. "I walked all through the Abbey ruins and no one insulted me or stabbed me—not a ghost, no shadows looming up,"—she flung out her hand—"not a bat to catch at my hair, not an owl even. Only children playing hide-and-seek."

"Not at this time of night," he said sternly. "And you said you were not going *in* anywhere." He fanned the air as if in disgust.

"It was only a *country* pub," she assured him. "Everything all right here? Oliver all right?"

"It seems so odd," he complained, and he couldn't say worse than that, "married women cavorting about the countryside, going into pubs alone. Quite frankly, Julia, I hope you won't do it again."

"I did *not* cavort," she cried. "I just walked along, and

104

once sat on a seat to rest. Why should you think I was cavorting? I don't believe you even know what the word means. I'm damn sure I don't."

She exasperated him. Society necessarily has a great many little rules, especially relating to the behaviour of women. One accepted them and life ran smoothly and without embarrassment, or as far as that is possible where there are two sexes. Without the little rules, everything became queer and unsafe. When he had married Julia, he had thought her woefully ignorant of the world; had looked forward, indeed, to assisting in her development. But she had been grown up all the time; or, at least, she had not changed. The root of the trouble was not ignorance at all, but the refusal to accept. 'If only she would!' he thought now, staring at her; 'If only she would *accept*.' The room was between them. She stood there smiling, blinking still in the bright light. He was still fanning the air peevishly with his hand.

CHAPTER 12

SUMMER RAIN darkened the rooms entirely; not only the sheets of rain, but all the dripping foliage as well. The house seemed glued up: bannisters were damp to the touch, doors stuck, mahogany was plum-coloured and smeared, the stairs at intervals exploded. "And my heart feels stuck to my ribs also," Julia explained to the laundry-man, touching her blouse in a formal gesture. He leaned back and, scraping the bottom of his cup on the saucer, proceeded to drink. His white-topped cap lay on one chair, a greasy leather satchel full of coppers in another.

"Yes, it isn't nice," he said. "It swells up my ankles, the damp weather. Feels as if I'm walking on red-hot needles, sometimes." He was rolling down a black sock to display a palely freckled leg, when Roddy came in with the Wing Commander. Both Roddy and the laundry-man looked frightened.

For a second or two nothing seemed to happen, save the laundry-man sullenly dragging up his sock again, but at last a little girl edged her way into the room. 'My Felicity,' Julia thought at once.

"Well, I must push off," said the laundry-man, swinging his satchel over his shoulder and taking up the Davenants' dirty linen.

By this time, Roddy had decided on humour as the best reaction: Julia was teased accordingly, Felicity introduced and Oliver called from the conservatory where he was lying on an empty shelf reading, his book propped against a tin of Daisy-Killer and the rain dropping like bullets on the glass around and above him. Julia poured more hot water into the teapot and fetched some rather dusty Sèvres cups and saucers from the cabinet in the corner.

"As we were passing, I brought Felicity to meet Oliver," the Wing Commander explained.

The children steadily avoided one another's glance.

"I thought it would be nice for them to make friends," he continued.

'It will only be nice if it is nice,' Julia thought.

Roddy put down his cup. "Well, thank you for bringing me round, Davenant," said the Wing Commander, holding his own cup for more. Roddy could only linger for one wretched moment more, to ask if he should bring the car back later, to have his offer refused and to give one despairing look at Julia as he went.

Felicity drank tea, her face only half visible beneath a

thick black fringe, her hair falling in long sweeping fronds over her shoulders. Her brown hands with their pink nails held the valuable cup and saucer in clumsy anxiety. She accepted a heart-shaped biscuit and began to nibble it like a squirrel, turning it inquisitively and yet timidly in her hand between each bite. Oliver, who had finished his tea before the laundry came, stared up at Mrs Lippincote's bridesmaids as if he had never seen them before.

"Felicity will soon be coming to the Crescent every day," said the Wing Commander. "She is starting at Saint Winifred's in September."

"How nice," said Julia stupidly.

The heart was nibbled away, auricles, ventricles, sultanas and all. Julia offered another, but the black tangly hair shook negatively.

"Nice it may be," her father said. "They will try to stuff her head with Virgil and Pliny and Greek Irregular Verbs."

"All Greek verbs are irregular," Julia murmured.

"I think it nonsense. What use will it be to her when she leaves school? Will it cook her husband's dinner?"

"No, it won't do that, but it will help her to endure doing it, perhaps. If she is to cook while she is at school, then there will be that thing less for her to learn when she's grown-up: but, if she isn't to learn Greek at school, then she will never learn it afterwards. And learning Greek at school is like storing honey against the winter."

"But what use is it?" he persisted.

"Men can be educated; women must be trained," she said sorrowfully.

Under the cover of this conversation, the two children, with lids still lowered, ventured to contemplate one another, beginning at the feet.

"My mother," Julia went on, "begged me to look upon my education as a luxury, never to think of it as a way of

107

getting a good job, nor a good husband either, but only as a means of lessening my boredom if I did. And then," she added mournfully, " there is always the chance that Felicity may not marry."

The child brushed crumbs from her lap to the carpet and placed her feet over them.

" Your mother is alive still? " he asked stiffly.

" No."

" I'm sorry."

" Thank you. Actually, I never know quite what to say in answer to that. I've tried out several different things— ' It's all right ' and ' Not at all ' or ' Don't mention it '."

" I take it, it was a long time ago? "

" Yes. It was when I was a young woman. Oliver, is there nothing we can do to entertain Felicity? There are Mr Lippincote's bird books or the musical box in the maid's room. Are you fond of reading, Felicity? "

" Yes, thank you," said the little girl, but without enthusiasm.

" I think the musical box would be a great attraction," her father said in the robust tone of one who does not attempt to understand his children.

The two children went rather desperately from the room.

" They are quite at our mercy," Julia said. " How abominable of us."

" Children are better in one another's company."

She offered him a cigarette out of a squashed packet she found in her pocket. " Ah, now I think I have guessed what you used to be. The Headmaster of a little boys' Preparatory School. It would give you the air of authority mingled with despair ; and then, with the young masters falling in love so much with your wife, as they always do, you *would* have become dour and aloof. Now, wasn't it so? You have obviously been ' sir'd ' till you are sick and silly."

108

" All the same it wasn't so."

" You vow that? "

" I vow you are wrong."

" A pity, for I see it all so perfectly. Even the buildings, and little things like your taking your Bible from the head boy at Prayers, with a piece of purple ribbon to mark the Collect for the day. *Nothing* to do with schoolmastering? "

He shook his head.

" I shall try again. Will you say ' yes ' if I guess right? "

" No."

" Then let me try if I can make your expression change."

He folded his arms, a gesture occurring so often that she decided to search for it in *Jane Eyre* as soon as he had gone.

" A barrister? " He was silent.

" One of those actors in a repertory company that never quite make the grade, who play the parts of titled men and have their hair streaked a little with white liner above the temple. And are very English," she conceded.

He smiled.

" A poultry farmer, then? "

" That is what officers do *after* wars, not before them."

" Oh, well, I give up. I shall think of some more in bed to-night and we will play the game another time. Are you, by any chance, a Mason? "

" No, why do you ask? "

" I thought if you were, you might be interested in a little book of Mr Lippincote's I found. It is in manuscript, but quite entertaining. It tells you how to do initiation ceremonies and how to make a Past-Master or whatever it is. A great deal of assing about with symbols; in fact, just what one would expect."

" But surely that is all secret and should never be left lying about? " The Wing Commander, Mason or not, believed, on the whole, in men hanging together.

"Poor Mr Lippincote could not help dying. Death does not always give us a chance of tidying up."

"You must have known you were not meant to read it."

She laughed in delight. "But *I* have nothing to be loyal to. Will they try to make me a Mason, then, like the woman who hid in the grandfather clock? I always despised her for being bought. I would have exposed the whole thing in a letter to *Time and Tide* and made them invent something new. They hide it from us because they know that they are being rather silly and that we should laugh. This book makes that obvious."

"I don't suppose that what you found was in the least important, but it wasn't honourable of you ..."

"Oh, men and their baby games!" she cried.

"You are a very inquisitive woman, and rather mischievous as well."

"To myself, I seem like a little point of darkness with the rest of the world swirling in glittering circles round me. How I *long* to draw some of the brightness to me! That is what makes me inquisitive—it is only stretching out my hands to other people. Yes, it has made me that. I hope it will never make me mischievous. But perhaps it has. Roddy has often begged me to stop. It embarrasses him when I try to overhear conversations in restaurants, or sit and stare with my mouth open in the train, and what good does it do, since other people's lives remain an illusion? You may catch at their clothes and are sometimes left with shreds of them in your hands, but the people themselves are gone and then what little treasure and brightness you may bring home to yourself" (and again she touched her blouse as she had done before) "changes at once to darkness, is absorbed by your own shadow."

"You must forgive me. In my heart, I know you to be

110

the least mischievous of women. Yet Roddy gets cross with you?"

"Aren't you being sly now? Did I say that?"

"I thought you implied it."

"Ah, did I, though? I will not have your words put into my mouth." She went over and drummed on the window with her knuckles. The rain slanted down, looking green against the green wet heart-shapes of the lilac leaves. The privets were like sponges, the gravel brilliant. "You can't take Felicity back in this. Let her stay. Send for her later."

"You are sending me away?"

"You have had your tea. You have brought your daughter. You have . . ."

"Oh, hush! I have annoyed you. You will hear nothing against Roddy. Is that it?"

"I will hear nothing against Roddy. Nothing."

"Come back. Don't turn away from me. In real life people may be allowed to sit and talk for hours without moving. There is no audience to complain. No need for you to go upstage and look out of the window."

In a muffled way, she said: "There *is* need."

He went upstage also and put an arm round her, which is perhaps the best we are able to do for those who weep too easily.

"Don't turn to shadow because I draw near to you," he implored. "I know this—you think me a ridiculous figure, stiff with my own dignity, acting a melancholy but undistinguished role, falsely romantic. All right. But if I am a poseur, I am not at the same time a hypocrite. I have never deluded you, nor myself, nor anyone who is real. I feel responsible for bringing you here. I persuaded Roddy to find a house"—surprise put an end to her sniffing—"because in this sort of job—office jobs, schoolmastering, nurse-maiding—it settles an officer to have his wife. We are

not combatants and do not give up our lives, or need to do so, in the same way." He withdrew his arm while she blew her nose. "But I have interfered wrongly. I have had a hand in bringing you here, and now you are not happy. Roddy is a good officer, but it is you I care about now. If I could help you . . ." He held up his hands, palms towards him, as he spoke, examined them closely but as if without hope and put them out of sight in his pockets. A schoolmaster's gesture, she noted, at the end now of her grief.

"If," he continued, "if there is something about this particular place which makes you miserable, and Roddy would agree, I would do what I could to get him shifted. Even . . . no, I was going to say, even if he would *not* agree, but I don't think . . ." He floundered, having gone farther than he intended, a stroke at least too far.

"Come, we are friends now," she said. "And I will stay on here, if you please. Why, I could not leave Mrs Lippincote just yet." She smiled up at the wedding group. "I have never met her, but she has cast a net of anxiety over me. No. When I want to go, it will be up to Roddy to ask you. If he wishes. I have no right to be considered. No one asked me to come."

"I asked for you."

"Yes. That surprises me a little." But he thought she was being careful to give him no chance of explaining.

"Let's find the poor children." At the door, she laid a hand on his arm. "I don't apologise to friends about crying. I'm afraid it has always been a thing we do easily in my family. People get used to it."

.

The musical box had clicked out *Boccherini's Minuet, The Blue Bells of Scotland*, and was now tinkling unsteadily

through something called the *Stephanie Gavotte*. Felicity, sitting on the maid's bed, on a rust-marked mattress, a pile of thin blankets and a lumpy bolster, had listened politely to the first two tunes, but now grew restive. Oliver stood by the musical box, one hand in his trousers' pocket, the other laid formally on the bedside table, as if he were having his portrait painted.

Felicity swung down from her perch. "What is this?" she asked, walking all round the dressmaker's dummy.

"It is a lady called Madame Héger."

Felicity bowed.

"At night, she creeps into our bedrooms and looks at us asleep and into our pockets and drawers. My mother has seen her at it."

"A spy, then?" Felicity hit her on the bosom. "Do you like musical boxes?"

"No," said Oliver.

"No more do I. There isn't anything you can do with them. Only listen. And wirelesses are better for that. I think we've had it on enough." She looked nervously at the door. "What do you like doing?"

"I don't know. Reading. What do you?"

"Fishing. I go nearly every day, but I'm forbidden, so I have to tip the fishes back in when it's time to go home."

"Why?" asked Oliver stupidly. "Oh, I see."

"I have nowhere to keep them where they wouldn't be found."

"You could keep them here," said Oliver. "You could keep them in the conservatory. And come and see them every day. I would give you a shelf for your own."

In her excitement she clasped her arms round Madame Héger until she rocked, and she laid her cheek against the sloping bust. "When can I start? Before they come, tell me when I can begin."

" To-morrow, if you like."

" What is that bell ringing? "

" It's at the school."

" Oh, yes." Her face changed, grew dreamy, clouded and then cleared. " To-morrow, then. I could even have a net, if you would keep it for me. All I have now is a jam-jar I hide under the bush at the river."

" Where does your mother think you go to? "

" Oh, to Olive Fielding's. To play. As if I'd play with that little liar! "

Oliver had the look in his eyes, and the same twitch at his lips, which he kept for his mother.

" Who is Olive Fielding? "

" Oh, the Fieldings. You know. Her father's a Regular."

" What does that mean? "

She looked surprised. " It means they do it always war or peace," she said coolly.

" What does *your* father do in peace? "

" Look! She's going to faint! " Madame Héger rocked uncertainly, but Felicity steadied her. " She hasn't got a face and yet she looks angry. That's funny. Fancy your chest being able to look angry! Oh, he was a dentist," she said indifferently. " I've forgotten. Except going for rides in the chair. I've forgotten lots of things about before the war— our house where we used to live—I can't even remember which way the bath went—and ice-cream and bananas. And I don't see how I'll ever be expected to eat them," she said in her mother's voice, " considering that they're an acquired taste."

Just as Julia and the Wing Commander reached the door Madame Héger fell flat, knocking down the maid's soap dish and breaking it in two.

CHAPTER 13

"BEAUTIFUL FORMATION," Felicity murmured, lying on her back at the edge of the river. Oliver looked up, too. White the Fortresses looked, spread out across the milky pearly sky.

"Fine aircraft, too. I'll hand that to the Yanks," said Felicity generously, rolling back on to her stomach.

"What kind are they?" Oliver inquired.

Her eyes stretched in surprise. "Forts, of course. Now this one, coming this way—that's a Dakota."

"It's the sort of shape of a moth," Oliver suggested. She acquiesced; for, flying over—and its very shadow passed over their faces—it did look blunt-headed, wings sloping back, a little like—"a yellow under-wing," said Felicity, always, apparently, exact. "But moths look like that when they're still, not when they're flying."

"There is a moth called a Four-spotted Footman," said Oliver.

"I know. I once had an Elephant Hawk, a very large moth, wing-span so big." (She measured six inches between her hands.) "Pink and pale-green, white fur on its legs. My mother made me throw it away. She's afraid of them."

Oliver, that credulous little boy, thought he would have been, too.

"And that's a Tiger," she added, as a Dominie crossed the horizon.

It was a fine hot day at last, but the grass was dampish and made their thin clothes feel sticky against them. The river was empty. Oliver thought how it is difficult to enjoy a holiday if other people are enjoying themselves too: others must be toiling and sweating, or at least out of the way.

He had always thought Bank holidays useless, a wasted day for everyone.

Felicity put her brown hand down into the river, the water wavered through her fingers, numbing them. The hand became something different from the rest of her, as if life stopped short at the wrist, the icy water gripping her viciously. She leaned over farther to watch her face trembling in reflection; little ripples broke across it, shot it into a kaleidoscopic pattern and then, as the water smoothed again, the face reassembled, pale above the brown weeds. Beneath her, along the bank, were rat-holes in the yellow clay, clumps of iris and borage and forget-me-nots. Little tarnished fishes swept along and at some inexplicable signal flicked round in unison and streamed back the way they had come. Her long dark tangly hair trailed now on the water. She caught at the sharp, silken weeds. In the water, bloodlessly, a little white cut opened in her finger, but when she took it out the blood gathered and fell in brilliant beads. She sucked her finger. The taste was rough, like ink or cheap wine; her hand felt smooth and beautiful from the water. She was completely happy. Every day at tea time, she would watch her glass filled with milk, the shape of the glass slowly growing white until the brim was reached and then she would always sigh with pleasure. Now, her heart was filled to the brim with contentment and there was the same sensation of simple pleasure. Still sucking her finger, she asked: " Are you an only child? "

" Now I am. Once I had a baby sister, but she died as soon as she was born."

Felicity frowned.

" Why do angels bother with bringing them just so that they can die? I can't see any sense in it."

Neither could Oliver, who thought that there was some aspect of religion so far unrevealed to him.

" And did it have a coffin? A very small one, I suppose."

"I don't know. I never would like to ask my mother. It doesn't seem quite polite."

"They bury babies in white coffins lined with white velvet," said the knowledgeable Felicity.

"Do you wish you had a brother or sister?" asked Oliver.

"One wouldn't be any use."

"It would make it better at Christmas, even one would make *that* better. It wouldn't be three grown-ups trying to give one child a nice time."

Felicity peered at her jam-jar hidden in the cool darkness of the long grass. Half-a-dozen red-throated fishes with sequin eyes darted round a piece of weed in the yellowish water. "Ah, my darlings!" she cried, and covered them up again. "It must soon be time to go home. I wish I could get some water lilies before I go."

"We could never reach them," said Oliver with indifference. He was lying there with the grass tickling his nose, thinking of *The Wind in the Willows*, a book he had read when he was a child.

"Further down they're nearer the bank." She wandered away from him, along the river's edge. The sun beat through her shirt between her shoulder-blades. She was drowsy with the sound and smell of the river; plantains whipped against her bare ankles. A swan drifted along, seemed blown by the wind, turning its neck, to left, to right, like a royal personage passing down the ward of a hospital.

She called Oliver to help her. Lying on the bank, he held on to her legs while she wriggled forward, grasped the long slippery stalks which slid through her fingers. She pulled some, little yellow knobs on slim stems, almond-smelling. "A few more!" she cried, and slipped. Face-down in the water, she could feel Oliver tugging still at her legs, pulling hard. Grazing her face against the bank, she was dragged to safety at last, a few yellow buds clutched in her hands.

Oliver took out his handkerchief and rubbed her hair, but the handkerchief became sopping wet and the hair no drier.

" I shall get into awful trouble at home," she moaned.

" You will have to come to my house first. My mother will help you."

Kneeling on the grass beside her, he wiped traces of slime from her forehead. Her face was pale and wet and her eyelashes stuck together. She took off her shirt and wrung it out. They did not laugh, as grown-ups would have felt obliged to do, but did what they could with perfect gravity. She put on Oliver's flannel jacket and, carrying the jam-jar and the lilies, they set out for home. Water dripped from the hem of her shorts down the back of her legs.

They walked in silence mostly, but once she suddenly said : " I don't care," and then again, after a while : " Thank you for saving me."

' I have had an escapade,' Oliver was thinking. ' I shall always have this escapade to look back on, like father talking about when he was a boy.'

Roddy, walking back to lunch across the Crescent, was not pleased at the sight of Oliver in his braces, carrying a jam-pot, and in the company of a damp and grubby little girl with tangled hair.

" What have you been doing ? " he asked, as they met at the gate.

" Running wild," said Oliver with beautiful simplicity, putting his arm along Felicity's shoulders protectively.

CHAPTER 14

"To-day the expending of powers . . ."

"On the ephemeral pamphlet and boring meeting," Eleanor remembered, shifting cautiously on her hard chair, moving her weight from one buttock to the other. Her friends, absorbed as they were, had no need to quote Auden to themselves; or she supposed that was so, looking from one intent face to another, and at the fountain-pens going from left to right across innumerable notebooks. 'It's really my back-ache,' she thought, and then—with a sudden turn of honesty or humour or masochism—'I should make a good revolutionary, if it were not for my back. I am willing to die for my beliefs, as someone else once said, but I forget who, but not to-day. Not till my back is better.'

The descriptions of life in Bombay plainly bored her and, looking round at the alert faces of Kirsty, of Leo and Sarge (but Sarge was frowning at his knuckles, which he was examining with an air of outraged astonishment), of Vera, Eleanor was ashamed. It took an atrocity to shake her out of boredom. She was horrified to hear of Hindus tied to trees by their hands, their toes barely touching the ground, hanging there in the ferocity of the sun, a punishment, for— and this was the point—trade-union activity. She felt the pain of it in her own armpits, felt her ribs straining apart and her toes searching madly in her shoes. Yet the faces of the others remained unperturbed, remained merely alert. Sarge rubbed his thumb up and down his nose. The man next to her wrote the word 'victimisation' in his notebook in indelible pencil. 'They are quite used to it,' she thought. 'To them it is not a shock, but a logical conclusion, the con-

clusion to all they have known and learnt and scribbled in their notebooks.'

At the end of the room—and it was very much like a little white-washed Sunday School—Lenin, leaning slightly forward, pointed upwards with one hand, giving an impression, perhaps correct, of crowds surging beneath him. Then there were others: William Morris, she felt she recognised, and either Karl Marx or Ibsen, but of course Karl Marx (she blushed), and another very historical-looking man, wearing a night-cap. Her eyes, after their furtive wandering, assumed the proper look of expectancy, fixed determinedly on the platform; for surely the meeting could not last much longer?

Leo thought: ' The sun beating down, the veins swelling, the blackness coming up in waves, coming up to strike at the eyes. Stop!' Looking coolly before him at the table on the platform, the glass of water, the man with his thumb in his waistcoat arm-hole, the sensation of tears yet stung at the bridge of his nose. ' That's what's soft about me,' he thought. Concealed in his pockets, his finger-nails drove in, now here, now there, against his palms. ' It's what makes me soft at the core, and inefficient. Helpless and inefficient. Taking on too many burdens, one becomes a burden oneself. Taking on the burdens of other men's suffering. Never die other men's deaths, lest one grows unfit for one's own. A coward. Not to be a coward and yet not to become too brutalised. An acquaintance with brutality coarsens one or gives the last nudge over the edge of sanity. We can never remain ourselves when it happens. Only Sarge might.'

Kirsty thought: ' How much longer, Lord? If only there's milk at home, I'll have a plate of cornflakes for my supper. That's what I feel like. Ever since he got on the District Committee, he won't stop talking. Likes the sound of his own voice more than I do.' She placed a little blob of spit at

each end of a ladder which had begun to run from the knee down. 'O Lord, how much more? And there's all the duplicating when we get back.'

Sarge thought: 'Thirty-seven people. Three more than last week, but not enough. Apathy among the Forces about India? "Always count the audience," old Tom used to say. "Never come from a meeting without knowing how many."' Mentally, with affection and emotion, he saluted that figure from his past, who had taught him the larger part of what he knew and, only now, across the gap of years and death, was truly valued.

Vera wrote: 'Average Expectation of Life. Infant Mortality. Percentage Educated. Beri-beri. Syphilis, etc.' She then added 'Occupational Diseases' and followed it by a large question mark to indicate a little matter to be cleared up later in discussion, something she had somehow missed, and indeed the speaker did frequently slur over the middle syllables of words, particularly the names of diseases, of which there were naturally many. She drew neat lines under the main headings and was astonished to see the speaker sitting down and, with a mixture of modesty and nonchalance, taking a sip or two of water, and more astonished still when she looked at her watch and found that it was eight-thirty and Sarge already on his feet proposing a vote of thanks and throwing open (he made a gesture of it) the meeting to discussion.

Eleanor, at this, shrunk down, her bowed head symbolising anonymity, into the uneasy English silence in which no one would be the first to speak. She was wrong, though, for Vera was ready with her polite, studious question.

'Oh, answer! Don't make another speech!' Kirsty thought savagely.

As soon as people began to creep out at the back to catch buses, Sarge slowed down the momentum, so that the meet-

ing could be neatly rounded off, tied up like a parcel and laid on a shelf with all the ghosts of other meetings; only a few words of it remaining in the minds of Vera and her kind, a few emotions roused and subdued, a page or two written (but scarcely to be re-read) and Kirsty with a ladder in her stocking. 'Oh, is he coming back with us, then?' she wondered, gazing with apprehension at Sarge and Vera welcoming the speaker. 'That means the meeting going on till midnight. Eleanor, as well, it looks like. It's goodbye to the cornflakes, then. And the cheese is full of blue spots and covered with fluff, and the tin of pilchards hasn't got a key.' "Good evening, comrade," she said, holding out her hand to him and smiling, for there is hypocrisy in most circles. 'I'll have a go at it with a tin-opener, or Leo can. But it's turning it round at the corners is so difficult.'

By now they had drifted out on to the pavement, in the very shadow of the gasometer. Kirsty could never get used to the smell. She held her handkerchief to her face and, putting her other hand into Leo's, they sauntered on ahead. Vera walked along with the speaker, her head bent, her thin arms folded across her chest, a slight frown between her eyes, as she straightened first one little problem, then another. So Eleanor was left with Sarge. He locked up carefully and turned to her and smiled. "Well, Eleanor, you'll be asking for your card next."

This made her feel sought-after.

"I can never do that."

He put the keys in his pocket and they turned homewards along the shut-up street, reflected, as they passed, in navy-blue blinds at shop windows.

"Apart from Roddy, there is the other thing," she continued. "There is the motive. It is more or less an accident that I stumbled upon you all. There's nothing in my experience to make me take such a step. I feel it would

be an affectation, not altogether trustworthy. I don't think you can understand. You've worked in factories all your life. I've never been inside one. I've been treated with consideration by everybody, never victimised." The word ran easily off her tongue. "No, never victimised."

"So you are well satisfied with the world?" he said artfully.

"No. Not satisfied at all. Not with other people's worlds, nor even with my own. I'm lonely, like all my kind. The thing I notice about you all is that you're never lonely. You get tired, you argue, quarrel even, but you aren't lonely and, underneath, you all love one another and depend on one another and give one another courage. That's what life should be like, it seems to me. The pattern of your lives is interlaced, woven together." And she locked her fingers to show him what she meant. "The other way of living, the way I live, the way Julia lives, seems so completely senseless; shut away in air-tight compartments. The hours pass, but that is all one can say. The time goes by and things change, but nothing is really added to one."

"The motive of wanting life is as worthy a one, surely, as the motive of wanting equal pay, or employment or a chance of peace for one's children," he suggested. "Come in and have some tea." For they had reached number twenty-one and Leo and Kirsty had already gone in and Vera's voice could be heard on the stairs, explaining gently but firmly—yet what precisely she explained they could not hear. Only the words 'birth-rate' and then 'death' floated back to them.

Down below, in the kitchen, Kirsty searched for the tin-opener, but Leo knew just where it was and began gently and methodically to open the tin of pilchards. Water droned into the kettle, the gas sprang alight in a blue and yellow crown; bread was found, the cheese rejected.

"They keep coming down from the Committee," Kirsty grumbled, "and they never bring any rations. It's always *our* marge, even *our* butter, Vera's so goddam vague. Now, of course, there's not a scraping of anything to put on the bread." She flopped the pilchards into a glass dish. With the empty tin in her hand, she suddenly stopped her cussing, and, looking up, saw Leo, half-leaning against the gas-stove, smiling at her. She put the tin on the draining board and went over to him, reached up, her arms clasping him and her forehead resting against him.

"Leo, love me."

Again the sensation of tears between his eyes.

He raised her face, her chin in his hands. The freckles above her cheek-bones were golden, the skin faintly foxglove colour, even the greenish pupils of her eyes were flecked with gold. He tried to think quietly, to ease away the imminent tears. He imagined ferns growing, the golden seeds like scales, foxgloves, the feel of flower-petals, the coolness of them curling to the fingers, bees lost in the sensuous depths of hollyhocks, drunk under the translucent hoods of the fox-gloves. How beautifully, he thought, the light must be shed through the petals of a flower. Only the bees know it and they are blundering drunk with lust.

"You do love me, Leo?"

Only Kirsty and Sarge asked him questions. The others spoke so that no answers were necessary. The women, Eleanor, for instance, would never address him directly, only include him in the general conversation by sometimes smiling dutifully at him.

"I've made you smell of pilchards," Kirsty said, sniffing his jacket. Her own fingers were fishy. They smiled, but in the midst of her laughter she grew tense against him, went rigid, 'all ribs and elbows,' he thought, 'like a child.' Then they heard Sarge crashing downstairs. He always came down

124

sideways because the stairs were narrow, hopping down, two steps at a time.

"The kettle's boiling," said Kirsty, winding her handker-chief round the handle and lifting it from the stove.

"Good. Look, Eleanor's going to stay the night, as well as Phil. She'll have missed the last bus."

Kirsty wasn't particularly interested. She placed the lid on the teapot. Leo hadn't moved, but he was frowning now. He took the tea from her and went upstairs.

She felt Sarge's scrutiny and began to fuss, picking up the bread knife and laying it down again, behaving rather idiotically in her confusion.

"If you could spare a blanket," he was saying. Certainly the words were there, hung almost tangibly between them, but were nothing to do with the thoughts of either and did not correspond to the look in their eyes.

"You alarm me, Kirsty," he said quietly.

"I alarm myself," she mumbled, looking down at the draining board.

"What about Leo?"

"If my loving worried him or alarmed him, I'd stop. I could do that. I could do anything that was necessary."

"Would you know?"

"I'd know all right," she cried. "It's my chief thing, I tell you. I don't just love him as you do. I . . . I'm staked on him."

"I know. That's why you alarm me." He sighed. "It'll be all right about the blanket then?"

Each carrying some of the supper things, they went upstairs.

.

Eleanor had slipped round the corner to the call-box. Lifting the receiver, she had begun to tremble. Roddy's

austere voice at the other end did nothing to calm her, as she forced in coins and began to quaver at him. "Hallo? Roddy?"

"Yes," he said with impatience.

"Look! I'm not coming home." ('What made me say "look"'? she wondered. It meant, 'I am about to tell a lie.') "I'm staying the night with Threlly. I came out to telephone," she ran on wildly (for the distance between number twenty-one and the call-box was nothing. No time to sort the facts out ready), "because, because I don't want her to hear. Cowper's away for the night and Threlly's nervous. So I shall go back. She won't admit . . ."

"O.K.," said Roddy tiredly. "I expect you're really on the loose," he added, with the gallantry he supposed she would require of him. "Good-night."

"These school-teachers," he said, as Julia crossed the hall. "Eleanor's not coming back. A lot of fuss about some old girl being frightened and another old girl doing this and that. Why the hell I'm supposed to be interested . . ."

.

Now Eleanor lay on the sofa in the front sitting-room. She felt stuffy, yet cold; exhilarated, yet depressed. Her head was on an old cushion, her body weighed down under Kirsty's blanket and Sarge's great leather coat from his motor-cycling days. It was a very heavy coat and the leather of it creaked when she moved. She moved a great deal, feeling chilly and uneasy, strangely excited, so that it seemed impossible to sleep. When she shut her eyes, she could hear more plainly than ever, Roddy's cold voice answering her, her own breathless voice reeling off lie after lie. 'I can't live up to him,' she thought. 'I never could as a child. He was always braver and nobler, forgave people, never told lies,

126

gave up his toys. He always was and always will be. That's the truth. And if he ever found out about to-night, I'd die.'

The sounds of running water had at last ceased, the house grew quiet. Up on the mantelpiece, the famous clock ticked and rustled and even, on occasion, struck, preceded by a whirring like the sound of angels' wings. 'Everything so strange,' she thought. 'Who am I? Lying here, under this coat, which is heavy but certainly not warm. It is not I. Or is it, at last, I, myself? The adventurer, the liar, the hypocrite?'

But in spite of all the harsh words, she smiled as she put out an arm and tucked one sleeve and then the other under her back and, falling asleep as it were in the embrace of Sarge's empty sleeves, the smile was still upon her lips.

CHAPTER 15

RODDY KISSED Julia and went off to a party in the Mess —a men's party, a 'presence required' party, he explained, leaving the house with a look of resignation. Watching him go, she was interested to see, as he turned for a second to latch the gate, the change that had come over him; gone the forbearance, and in its place geniality and a look of anticipation.

She turned from the window, feeling depressed. Eleanor was still at her supper, licking a greasy finger, absorbed, her plate full of artichoke leaves. When first she had come to live with them, Julia had been flattered at this absorption in food; but after a while, repelled; and now angered. 'I, too, love

food,' she thought, wandering round the room, putting this straight and that crooked, ' but it doesn't make me absent-minded.'

She turned the wireless a little louder, then very loud. A Bach sinfonia. She stood at the window again, tapping a foot, wagging her head. Wrens flew with a flicker of pale colour in and out of a bush which was fluffy with raspberry-pink blossom. The blossom which had faded was ginger. The red-hot-pokers were the palest of illuminations. Golden privet was unremitting in its attempt to cheer.

Eleanor took up her plate of discarded leaves and went out, annoyed about the Bach. When she heard the clatter of crockery, the violent rush of water, Julia was obliged to follow. She dried the dishes in silence.

When they were finished, Eleanor settled at the dining-table, unscrewing her fountain-pen glumly, and deciding that since she would be greatly relieved once her long overdue letter to Germany was written, she would deal with it quickly.

' Dear Reg,' she wrote—it was as well that her fluctuations were a matter of indifference to Reg himself. She wondered what on earth she could follow up with. He had been Stella to her Swift, the victim of her unburdenings, another side of her own nature. But he did not answer back, except on a postcard at irregular intervals, without unburdening himself except about the cold (real to him, but uninteresting to her) and with no indication that he might detect a Vanessa crossing her pages, or any distraction which might be the cause of her writing ' Dear Reg' so tersely.

" How you do moon about," she said to Julia.

" If we ever leave this house, I shall take this with me," Julia said. It was a white china swan on the mantelpiece and she had filled the hollow between its wings with sweet-williams.

" Julia ! "

"Oh, it's only a cheap thing. We had one in the nursery when I was a child."

"What you didn't have in the nursery was someone who could bring you up properly."

Julia said a rude word. Then—"I'm off," she said suddenly. "I'm not hanging about like a woman in a book for my husband to come home drunk. There's only one answer to that, and that's a conventional one, a vulgar one, the rolling-pin one, and I can't do it."

"I've seen Roddy come home from a great many parties, but never drunk. Could you say the same of yourself?"

"Oh, people get drunk in different ways—and remain sober in different ways. I'd rather be beaten than jollied."

Eleanor curved her lips and wrote: 'I hope the cigarettes arrived and that you are well,'—a bleak enough little sentence to chill anyone's heart. 'How horrible to have had ear-ache,' she continued. 'I hope . . .'

"I'll go to the pictures," said Julia.

"*Wuthering Heights* is on."

"Oh, God, no!"

'. . . that it is quite better now,' Eleanor wrote.

Julia had run upstairs, was pulling out drawers in a frenzy, but closing none of them; there was scarcely time.

'I hope this . . . I hope that,' Eleanor wrote, with indifference.

.

She walked in the Abbey ruins for half-an-hour, but Mr Taylor did not come. 'An assignation,' she thought, strolling down a cloister. 'We should have had an assignation. In the Dormitory, by the clump of valerian, at eight-thirty. We ought to have written notes to one another. I expect he writes in green ink, sloping backwards, on deckled-edged paper with imitation rain-spots all over it.' She imagined

Roddy's disgust, handing her just such a letter at breakfast time.

The river slid by; lovers crunched along the gravel walks; snatches of boring talk came from them. "It isn't as if it was the expense," said one girl, and . . . "standing in the rain for . . ." grumbled another. The young men said nothing. They leaned against the girls and breathed. From the other side of the river, a very depressing sound, the Town Band, was wafted across in occasional gusts.

Julia took courage and walked towards Mr Taylor's bungalow. She was a little nervous about going there on her own, but wanted a drink. 'A brandy this time,' she decided.

A little girl went by with a broken fishing-net, bawling "I want to . . ."

"You would!" her mother cried after her. "Well, you can't here, that's all. You should have thought of it before."

As Julia turned in at the gate, she could hear the woman still shouting: "You'll have to manage, that's all." Going up the path, she trembled with fury; stalked into the silver passage and into the room, where half-a-dozen people turned to stare at her.

This time, Mr Taylor stood behind the bar and Miss Warburton sat on a stool surrounded by officers of medium rank. She noted Julia's approach without recognition, stared coolly when she was wished 'good evening', then asked: "Are you a member of the Club?"

"Greta!" murmured Mr Taylor. "Good evening, madame." He stood there helplessly, separated from her by all the bottles and glasses, looking ill and undignified. "What will you have to drink?"

"Excuse me, but I asked are you a member here."

"Greta, please!"

Glance in his direction she would not.

"No," said Julia.

"Sorry, but unless . . ."

"I came to see Mr Taylor."

"Charlie's on duty."

"Oh, no, he bloody isn't." And he threw a glass cloth down to show what he was about. Julia, stimulated rather than mortified by this scene, favoured violence. 'If only Roddy could see!' she thought. Mr Taylor had knocked over a half-filled glass and the beer began to trickle. He dropped a swab on the little puddle and lifting the bar-flap came round into the room. Miss Warburton sat with bowed head, twisting a ring on her finger, as if something of doubtful taste were going on and she would consider raising her head only when it was all over. Julia waited with interest. The officers tried to breeze over the commotion with suggestions for more drink.

"Oh, no," said Mr Taylor with enormous gravity. "No more. There must be no more."

Julia felt he must be drunk.

"I have caused quite a little scene, so I think I will be going," she said loudly. Miss Warburton turned her ring, breathed on the large oval stone and polished it on her velvet cuff.

"Good-night, Mr Taylor."

"No more," he said distractedly.

At the door it was all she could do to resist clicking her heels, bowing herself out. Passing between the dingy balloon-fabric, she found that the air outside was a pleasure to breathe.

"Ah, wait! wait!" And Mr Taylor crossed the lawn after her with a bottle and a couple of tumblers in his hands. When he came level with her, he was all to pieces. 'He is dying,' she thought.

131

His clothes were now fringed and frayed, and the hand that went up in a nervous movement to his mouth, in an attempt to conceal a broken tooth, was not clean.

'They are the hands he started out with,' she suddenly thought. 'Like all of us. Our faces, our bodies change, our manners, our hearts, but not our hands.' She found herself looking at her own.

"Brandy!" he panted; but it was not the cry of distress she imagined it, merely an explanation of the bottle in one hand, the greasy tumblers in the other. "Madame, I . . . it is my wish you should . . ."

"You are tired. Is there nowhere for us to sit down?" She had almost reached the gate and looked about in vain for any seat.

"There is the summer house, if you will . . ."

They moved back across the dry-brown lawn. Surrounded by glassy laurel leaves was a little cave of tree bark and darkness.

'Who is who?' she thought tiredly. 'What belongs to what? And am I about to drink Miss Warburton's brandy?' For drink it she knew she would.

"The glasses . . ." he was saying in disgust. "I am ashamed . . ." And then, as if guessing her thoughts: "But it is my own brandy. I've carried it from place to place, never dreaming I should drink it in this way. . . ." He looked with horror at the cold sky, the leaves borne down by the wind, smothering their little shelter, and then, with the same look of weariness and distaste, he gazed at the two tumblers. "Nor that I should have the honour . . ." He bowed at her and then his face puckered. "She shouted at me," he said, setting the glasses down carefully between them on the slatted seat. "Get out! Get out!" His hands trembled. "It hurts me when women . . ."

"Who is she?" Julia asked in a low voice.

"A bitch. She is a bitch. Madame . . . I . . . forgive that . . ."

"It is what she appears to be. Will you please not call me madame any more. We are English people, aren't we? I am either Mrs Davenant or Julia."

'When *will* he broach the bottle?' she wondered.

"Romeo and Julia," he muttered. "Women think money buys everything. Greta thinks that. When you are ill, you know it isn't so, don't you?"

"I have never been ill."

"What is money?" he asked, looking at his fringed cuff. "What is ambition? She's beaten me. I see that. But what good can it do her? Here is the brandy. Not all her money . . . Christ knows . . . I'm sorry . . . *God* knows where she gets her money from. She doesn't like brandy. No, its gin-and-lime, gin-and-lime all the time with her."

'Here am I sitting in a summer house with the dregs of society,' Julia thought placidly, wondering what Roddy was doing at the moment.

"What are you going to do?" she asked, for she had given up all hopes of the brandy by now.

"I shall send for my sister. She'll make her go. Get out! Get out! I don't like being shouted at. It's my sister's house and she'll make her go."

The bottle was tilted and hovered at last above the tumblers. "Yes," he murmured, "disgusting glasses. Cold brandy. You love brandy, madame, that makes me most happy. Very few women really love brandy . . ."

Julia didn't know that she loved it as much as all that, but putting her lips to the glass she was certainly braced by the fumes of it, and the sip she took went at once to her heart, kindled beautifully and branched out its flames.

"And will your sister come?" she asked.

"Ah, that's what I ask myself."

133

"Who else is there?"

"My mother. There is always my mother."

The idea of him having a mother fascinated her.

"She is a Frenchwoman," he continued, with detachment. "A very beautiful woman—for her age, of course. So tiny that she has to wear children's shoes, size thirteens, black shiny leather with round toes." Julia unconsciously tucked her feet under the bench. "And she always has one of those lace shawls over her hair . . . white hair, naturally."

"Naturally," Julia agreed. 'What was dad then?' she was wondering. "What will happen when you go indoors?"

"I shall go to bed."

"But, this Greta . . .?"

"She'll have gone home, if I stay long enough." He looked with calculation at the colourless wash of darkening sky. "Yes, if I stay long enough, she'll have gone."

"But where to? Doesn't she live here, then?"

"Live here? Of course she could never do that."

"Oh, I see." Once, Julia, peering in at a lighted window as she passed down some street, had had curtains rattled across in her face, and now she was in the same confusion as then. Humiliation and defiance alternated in her. Then there was the brandy. That it was good brandy, was now established beyond doubt. Similes occurred to her constantly, of fires kindled, of flowers unfurling, of jewels burning and fountains flashing. Roddy, ranting and roaring, as she had supposed he would, at his men's party, was forgotten. She held the glass against her cheek thoughtfully, not that that could do much good, for her face was cool and her fingers quite cold.

"You live here alone then?"

"Until my sister comes."

"She *will* come then?"

"How not? She is my sister, isn't she?"

134

" Look, don't you think we had much better not have any more of this . . ."

" I see no reason . . ."

" But save some for another time."

" There never will be another time. You'll be careful not to come here again."

" I shall most certainly come. I shall come quite soon to find out how you are."

At this, covering his face with one hand only, he vomited up a few sobs, a tear or two fell through his fingers. Even in the gathering darkness she could see that, his wet fingers, and a tear running down inside his wrist into his sleeve. With a sensation of utter revulsion, she put her arm across his back and with awkward caresses, like a child, tried to comfort him.

.

The men, beer-cans on their heads, had begun a solemn ritual dance; with movements more appropriate to scarred and feathered savages, they chanted, bent knees, advanced, with solemn staring eyes. Roddy, who was not particularly good at this, glanced at the clock and finding that it was long past eleven, thought of Julia and slipped out unnoticed, as all but the bachelors and the most reckless of husbands had already done.

Disconcerting, the way the pavement seemed to vary in its distance from his lifted feet. With each step, he struck an unexpected level or plunged sickeningly into a trough. Railings went by, but he scorned to touch them. He wandered, rather than walked, along the pavement. There was also an annoyance with the door-key. He particularly disliked having Julia hear him fumbling at that job, but fumble and scratch about he did.

The hall seemed full of furniture, placed about at incon-

venient angles. Then suddenly the staircase filled with light and Eleanor was coming downstairs in a dressing-gown.

"Julia is not in yet," she announced, drawing a lapel across her bosom in a guarded moment.

After a moment, Roddy said : " I never knew she was out."

"She went to the pictures."

Between each remark there seemed to be a pause in which the ticking of a clock drew close to his ears and receded.

"What time do pictures stop ? " (Tick—stop, tick—stop.)

"Oh, ten o'clock at the latest nowadays."

"Well, what can I do ? "

"It's too late to ring people. Unless the police . . ."

"The police ? " He looked quite startled.

"Well . . . give her half-an-hour. I'll make some coffee." She disappeared, her dressing-gown still clutched defensively across her chest.

"Oh, bed ! " he groaned, covering his eyes with the palms of his hands.

"Only the hall is blacked-out," said Eleanor, when she returned with the coffee cups. They sat on the wide bottom stair, the tray between them. The coffee cleared his head a little, but only to allow doubt and bewilderment to crowd in. They could not account for her going out, staying out ; for she could easily have telephoned, they agreed. No matter where. . . .

"She gets such strange notions," they said, "and impulses."

"I am a little worried about Julia lately," said Eleanor. "She is moody and unlike herself."

Roddy suppressed the thought that Julia had been unlike herself ever since he had first known her.

"Her nerves," Eleanor went on, "are all to pieces. I feel very anxious for her."

"Well, I . . ." But she rode him down.

136

"Roddy, I hope you don't mind my saying so, but I feel she is drinking too much."

"Oh, I wouldn't say that," said Roddy generously.

"I do say it. I say it because I am fond of Julia and . . ."

"Naturally. Everybody . . ."

Julia, opening the hall door and finding them sitting on the stairs drinking coffee, was astonished.

"What *is* this?"

"Where have you been?" they cried.

She poured a little coffee into Roddy's empty cup and began to drink it. "Out," she said.

"But where? We've been worried."

"Are you the police?" she asked tiredly.

"Julia!"

"Oh, in the morning. By the morning I'll have thought up some explanation."

"We are not to have the truth, then?" Eleanor suggested.

Julia pushed by them and went upstairs. Half-way up, she turned and said: "Do you deserve the truth? That's what you must first ask yourselves. Before you begin to demand it from other people." Safe enough tactics. They both lowered their eyes.

CHAPTER 16

JULIA CARRIED the laundry-basket and a bowl of cold water into the dark, ferny kitchen and switched on the iron. The house was silent, except for the gurgling of the hot-pipes. Oliver had gone to tea with Felicity.

When the iron was nicely hot the door-bell began to ring.

Dratting like some old concierge, she went through the arch and along the passage. A silhouette suggesting height and gloom prepared her for the Wing Commander, not for the clergyman who stood there. 'High church,' she thought at once, noting his pallor and the emanation of conserved agony.

"Mrs Davenant?"

Bowing her head in acquiescence, she caught sight of her bare toes poking through the dirty quilted slippers which gaped now like codfishes.

"My name is Maffick."

"How do you do."

"I am taking the liberty of calling on you." In one thin hand he carried a sacred-looking book.

"Please come in."

'What on earth can I do with him?' she wondered. In the hall she smelt scorching and remembered the iron.

"I must just . . . one moment . . . excuse me."

"Not at all."

When she had switched off and turned the iron on end to cool, she found he had followed her into the kitchen.

"Please continue. I shouldn't like to hinder you."

"Well, it *is* rather a nice hot iron . . ."

"Please. I shall regard it as a compliment. If you will excuse me I will sit here by the window and talk to you."

'But what about?' she wondered, rummaging in the laundry-basket, rejecting a brassière as unsuitable and Roddy's pants as disloyal.

He admired the Adam's Blanket in the plant-pot and sat down.

The iron was too hot and she began to damp down the clothes, flicking water in all directions except Mr Maffick's. The drops rattled down on the dry linen like a shower of bullets.

138

"I am not a Christian, you know," she said as kindly as she could, not wishing anyone to waste time over her. He remained bland, with the infuriating calm of one who cannot be shocked. "But it is rude of me to talk shop," she added. He smiled, averting his eyes from the laundry-basket and therefore appearing smug.

"It is strange to be sitting in this kitchen once again," he mused. "But I must explain. This was my aunt Blanche's house. I am Mrs Lippincote's nephew."

This was not then a professional call, she decided, merely espionage.

The iron ran beautifully over Roddy's pyjamas-jacket, nosed into the pocket, turned, circled the buttons, only imperceptibly scorching the rose and pearl-grey stripes. With a tinge of malice, she shook out Eleanor's black lace knickers and spread them out on the ironing-board.

"As soon as the iron is cool, I shall make some tea," she promised. "Is the relationship on your mother's or your father's side? Oh, your mother's, of course. Fennester was the maiden name, wasn't it? Your mother was a Miss Fennester then?"

He was surprised at last.

"You haven't met my aunt yet?"

"No."

'That gossiping old charwoman, then,' he decided.

"I have met your cousin . . ."

"Phyllis?"

"Yes."

"Oh!"

"A charming girl."

His quick glance at her faltered. In his reluctance to meet her gaze, he found himself staring with fierce absorption at the black knickers. He thought they were vulgar, so did Julia. "The iron is still too hot and now I have scorched

139

the lace and my cousin will be cross with me," she said spitefully, although she had no motive for queering Eleanor's pitch with this strange clergyman.

The door-bell began once more.

"It must be my husband this time," she said. "He will have forgotten his key."

It was the Wing Commander. He came quickly into the hall and shut the door behind him, suggesting complicity.

"Julia, my dear!" He put an arm round her.

Now Mr Maffick appeared in the hall. "As your husband has come I will be off. I know that there is little chance for you to be together in these unhappy times . . ."

"I simply *have* to speak to Julia alone," said the Wing Commander, drawing her closer than ever to him.

Mr Maffick understood. Not only could he sense bad news, but also the nature of it. It would be difficult news to break to any wife, news of posting, as he supposed it was to be, to the Far East, tropical kit issued, fourteen days embarkation leave, and inoculation against yellow-fever. "I shall call again," he said. "And if ever you want me . . . if there is anything . . ."

Julia said, 'But' continually and without effect. Mr Maffick understood so quickly, his intuition informed him so definitely, that he merely wrung the Wing Commander's hand and was off, his own quiet agony answering theirs, as he softly closed the door behind him.

"But . . ."

"Julia!" His face was very white, very changed. She suddenly cried out "Oliver!" her eyes widening, burning with fear.

"He's hurt. There's been . . ."

"My God, he's dead."

"No, my dear. Hush! Of course, not bad like that. He's had a nasty fall and I've taken him straight to hospital. It

was the best thing to do, and then I came here at once to tell you. He'll be all right."

"Hospital! Where is he hurt?"

"Head. I'm afraid a bit of concussion and abrasions. He was climbing on the garage roof with Felicity and fell."

"But Oliver doesn't do things like that."

"Well, my dear, I'm afraid he did. I wish he had done it in any other house than mine. I mean I wish he had not done it at all—you must blame me dreadfully . . ."

"Oh, God, will he be all right?"

"I promise you. But it had to be hospital. They will find out all that's wrong. Now, please, you will be all right and brave and everything and I will take you there. The car's outside."

They both looked hopelessly at her slippers and then he sat her down on a chair and went upstairs. Oliver's room. No. Eleanor's room. No. He avoided the room with Madame Héger in and came at last to Roddy's and Julia's. In the wardrobe her white coat hung between Roddy's jackets. Those tunics with their faded rings on the sleeves brought the episode to its final level of unreality. He found a pair of sandals covered with fluff under the bed and went downstairs.

She was sitting still and shivering, her hands locked tightly in her lap.

"Where's Roddy?"

"Well, I'm afraid I'd sent him on an errand out of town. The whole thing's most . . ." he murmured incoherently, kneeling by her side, buckling the sandals. He put the coat round her shoulders and, taking a comb from his pocket, arranged her hair neatly behind her ears.

"You *shall* cry," he promised her. "But not until I say so."

She got into the car, and they drove down the Crescent.

'Not real!' she kept saying to herself, passing railings, trees, the Saint Winifred's Hotel. He apologised continuously.

"It was not your fault," she said, with bitterness. "It was mine. He didn't want to go to tea with you, but I made him. He always wants to back out of that kind of thing at the last moment and I wouldn't let him. I tied his tie for him and put him out of the front door. Now I wish I hadn't."

He touched her hand for a moment as he drove. Gravel crunched loosely beneath the tyres as they turned into the hospital between veronica bushes. Little cool dreadful smells came out of the entrance. They tiptoed nervously across black and white tiles.

A uniform does wonders in a hospital as elsewhere. They were led at once to the children's ward.

"Hello!" said Oliver brightly, sitting up in a bed which faced the door.

"Lay down, Oliver!" said the nurse.

"Oh, it is not as bad as you made out," cried Julia, turning accusingly as she embraced her son.

"It is not as bad as I had supposed it would be," said the Wing Commander with a strange mingling of relief and gloom. "But it was as well not to let you expect less trouble than there might be."

Beside Oliver's bed was a notice—"The Children may not be given Food during Visiting Hours." When Julia glanced up at it, he said: "It is like the Zoo."

His bedclothes dipped down to the floor, feathers came from his pillow, cotton-wool was slipping from his bandages which he kept pushing up above his eyes. The other children lay primly staring, averting their gaze when noticed.

"It has been an experience," said Oliver, flagging suddenly, his skin whitening.

"Well, tin-ribs," bustled the nurse. "Dear me, I can't have Mummies sitting on my beds." Julia stood up, but still

held Oliver's thin, blue-veined wrist. The Wing Commander looked round the ward, at the dim aquarium-light revealing dark green walls and whiteish paint and a vase of sulphurous dahlias.

"What is this for?" Oliver cried pettishly, pulling at the red mackintosh-sheet. "Do they think I am going to wet the bed?"

"I think it is just a custom," said Julia, who had never been in a hospital before. "Are you much hurt, darling?"

He tried to shake his head, failed, and put his hand up to the bandage.

"He'll be home to-morrow, I shouldn't wonder," said the nurse, tweaking smartly at his bed-clothes. "But home to *bed* mind!"

She moved away and Oliver signalled to Julia to come nearer.

"What do I do when I want to go to the lavatory?"

"Just ask the nurse for a bed-pan," Julia said.

The Wing Commander strode forward and whispered in Oliver's ear. Oliver nodded, looking first incredulous and then at peace.

"Well, now, Mummy and Daddy, I'm afraid it's time to shoo you away," said Nurse, bringing a thermometer in a paste-pot full of pink liquid.

"Why may I not take him now?" asked Julia.

"Patients can't be cleared until the House-Surgeon has made his rounds."

"And when will that be?"

"To-morrow morning. But in any case you'd have to make inquiries through Sister."

'What odd ways she has of expressing herself. What a strange preposition to have used in that case,' thought Julia, staring in wonder.

"Sister is the one done up in frills like a cutlet," said the

Wing Commander, tilting his head backwards in the direction of the door.

"Now, now!" said the nurse, becoming flirtatious with the enjoyment of his malice. "Daddies aren't allowed to talk like that."

"He is not my father," said Oliver.

"Nurse, it is time for Mr and Mrs Davenant to go," said Sister, disregarding rank in others and finding the oblique method of giving orders more fitting to her position.

"Goodbye, my love."

But he didn't wind his thin arms round her, only moved his head slightly on the pillow so that she could kiss his cheek and feel his dry, rough lips against her own.

"I shall be here first thing in the morning and I'll sit on the doorstep and wait for you."

He closed his eyes.

They clanked down the empty stone passages in some misery. A woman in labour was being carried in from an ambulance. She lay on a stretcher, her eyes quiescent with pain. 'When that's over, she will think for a little while that her trouble is finished,' Julia thought, still leaning, like a wife, upon the Wing Commander's arm. 'Then after another little while she will realise it has only just begun.'

"What time is it?" she asked as she got into the car.

He pointed to the clock on the dash-board and started the engine.

"But it can't be six o'clock!"

"It is, you know."

"What time will Roddy be back?"

"I'm afraid not until later."

"Oh, I see." She required the relief of talking to her husband, felt that to startle and alarm him would be to increase her own composure. "Which way is this?"

"The way I am taking you."

144

She was glad to see for once an end to the pavements. The stream of bungalows dribbled, failed, stopped. They began to drive through wide and undulating country, once (and this was the reason, she supposed, for so many elm-trees) the Parklands of the large stone houses they saw sometimes at the ends of drives, beyond gloomy lodges with dirty washing hanging round them and broken glass in the lamps above the wrought-iron gates. The parks were now patterned with corn-stalks, the draped and sculptured-looking sheaves full of shadows. Tractors whirred. Guns went off.

"We will get ourselves a drink," said the Wing Commander, slackening speed before a large road-house.

"But there is Roddy!" Julia cried.

"It could not be," said the Wing Commander, increasing his speed and leaving the road-house behind. "Roddy went in the brake."

"But why did we not have our drink?"

"We are going to." He swung recklessly into the side of the road before a little beer-house called 'The Cunning Man', where Hannah Kate Molesworth was licensed to sell ale and cider. He made a little speech before he got out of the car. "It is not a place I should bring most ladies to. It is merely a simple country pub, part of the root and backbone of England." (Julia glanced up with suspicion at these metaphors.) "But," he concluded, taking his hands at last from the steering wheel, "I thought you would like it, better than the vulgarity and artificiality of the other place, since you are a simple person yourself, Julia."

'I am not as simple as all this,' she told herself, but she only smiled and stepped out of the car. The pub was small and fusty inside, highly varnished and full of circling flies. There were white lace curtains and pink china beer handles painted with moss-roses. Against the bar leaned a couple of farm labourers, sunburnt and open-shirted. One of them

was the usual Irishman who stands by the bar of every pub selling talk for beer, one of the oldest professions. There was a tremendous smell of sweat.

They carried their beer to the bench outside.

"I always think I don't mind the healthy smell of sweat," said Julia, "but when I actually come to it, it seems so——" she shrugged and took a drink —"well, so . . . *un*healthy, perhaps."

Across the road men were carting wheat, the pitchforks glinting in the sun. One man stood on top of the load catching the sheaves. There began to be a sunset. Hens wandered before the inn-door, pecking half-heartedly at the weedy gravel.

"They make the best mothers," said the Wing Commander pointing.

"What, chickens?"

"No. Rhode Island Reds."

"Were you ever a farmer?" she asked with a pretence at innocence.

"God, no."

She smiled in despair. "Ah, this is pleasant," she said at last, surveying the placid landscape.

"I only wish you were happier."

"Yes, I wish that myself. There is always something with children."

"I sometimes wonder why women consent to have them. I couldn't help thinking on those lines when I saw that woman being carried into the hospital."

Sentimentality about motherhood always embarrassed her. She could only make light of it and speak as astringently as possible. "It is only that sort of talk which makes it bad," she declared. "Only a question of knowing what is to be expected of you. And the sort of ideas you have makes one expect the wrong thing."

146

"You speak from experience."

"I do indeed. It is a bloody business when you resist and the resistance is all due to sentimentality. When Oliver was born I resisted so insanely that all hope was lost for us both and I could do nothing more for myself. I suppose the first time one never does quite get the knack of it. There is *some*thing to be learnt, after all. The second time," (he looked surprised), "something came to me. I realised it was never meant to be pain, but sensation. How women *love* this sort of conversation. It's the only important thing we have. It has to make up for so much of life that men keep to themselves."

"Go on telling me. . . ." He waved his hand impatiently.

"My daughter's birth was so benign, only tiring in the exhilarating way that it is tiring to climb a hill to see a great stretch of country. Yes, greatly exhilarating and . . ." She wiped her mouth on her handkerchief and put her empty glass down on the seat . . ."an experience to look back on, that feeling of power and strength. That's how it ought to be. I can't help feeling . . ."

"But what happened to the child?"

"Oh, the child was dead in no time," she said in a shocking, light voice. "I will get some more beer," she suggested, putting her hand out for his glass.

But she was not allowed to be simple to that extent. When he had brought the filled glasses, he said : "I do you no good, I'm afraid."

"It wouldn't be nice at home this evening, without Roddy."

The sunset settled into long washes and ribbons of colour. A fleecy cloud like a swan with an azure breast slowly dissolved in the mackerel sky.

"If an artist painted a sky like that people would say he exaggerated."

She looked up doubtfully, but he was soberly enthusiastic and she drank her beer without the hope of a joke.

" I feel I want to be back home by the telephone," she said suddenly, and he saw that she had whitened round the mouth and nostrils and struck her hands together. He carried the glasses in and they turned away from the pub, that ' root-and-backbone ', she thought, ' of whatever it was he said.'

" And which way is this ? " she asked, as they drove away in an opposite direction.

" It is the other half of the circular tour," he announced. " I expect I could be cashiered for this."

" It would be the first time I had wrecked a man's career."

" It is the first time I care nothing for the consequences." In spite of this light-hearted statement, the gloom on his face did not shift one measure. Life had committed him too deeply to that habit. Not till he went to bed that night did he remember that she had not cried after all. He considered that remarkably brave of her, not knowing that Roddy, having borne with her intermittent weeping since supper, was at that moment turning over in bed, assuming the attitude of sleep and feeling she must now be left to cry herself out, for there was nothing more that he could do.

CHAPTER 17

OLIVER'S TEMPERATURE zig-zagged across the chart, so that he could not be allowed home the next day.

" Really, Mrs Davenant ! " said a stout and exasperated woman, who was the almoner, " your child is not the only one in this hospital."

"He is the only child of mine in the hospital," said Julia.

At lunch, "I have utterly failed him," she cried, pushing away some slices of tinned meat with a look of revulsion.

"For God's sake keep your sense of proportion," said Roddy.

"We are all sorry, but going without food will scarcely help matters," Eleanor explained, eating quickly to set a good example.

The next day, the whims, the caprices, the red tape, the irresponsibility, the vicious sadism and so on of the hospital allowed Oliver to come home. Roddy had time off to fetch him. He carried him out of the building to the taxi as if he were an infant. His legs hung down limply. He wore his bedroom slippers. His hair, which always grew so quickly, it seemed, when he was ill, hung in a silken fringe below the bandage.

"Now I have got you," said Julia.

"Don't make a fool of the boy."

"What was it like, darling?"

Oliver stared out of the window of the car as if he had not seen the outside world for many a long day. When he turned to Julia, he said: "I was afraid all the time of what they would do to me next, but I got out before they could do the worst thing of all."

"What would the worst thing be?"

"I kept hearing them say I would have to have my bowels opened."

"Oh, the terrors children suffer needlessly!" Julia cried. "It only means Syrup of Figs or something of that kind."

"I wish I had known," said Oliver simply.

As they entered the house he said: "It has made it seem more like my home, because I am coming back to it."

It was three o'clock in the afternoon and Eleanor was out. The summer holidays had begun, but she was at school

as much as ever. Unless she was somewhere else, which was the view to which Julia inclined.

Roddy agreed to carry Oliver once round the garden to inspect the growth of marrows, the length of runner-beans. It was as if he had been away for months, Julia thought, watching them go and feeling them to be for once truly father and son. They returned. Oliver had a bunch of striped York and Lancaster roses and Roddy a rough brown pear and a clove carnation for Julia.

Oliver was put to bed and Julia took up the tea and a special tray for Oliver, with a glass of milk, a plateful of bread and butter strips, a peach and a jar of sweet peas. Oliver surveyed the room and his tea with quiet contentment.

" The peach cost three-and-ninepence," his mother said, to increase his pleasure, not to diminish it.

" It has been worth every penny of it," he said, sucking the large wrinkled stone.

' How happy we are ' thought Julia. The sunlight reflected in her teacup danced on the ceiling. Oliver looked up and smiled. "Vanish, angel!" he said, as he had done as a baby, and from habit she placed her hand over the top of her cup.

"Well, I must get back and do some work or the Old Man will have something to say. He can't be a kind uncle to us all," said Roddy, patting Julia's head as he passed behind her chair.

She lay back sleepily, watching Oliver putting bread and butter fingers into his mouth one after another.

" What did you have for tea in there ? "

" Bread and lemon curd."

" No cake ? "

" Some of them did. What their mothers had brought them."

" Oh, I *am* sorry. It didn't occur to me. I thought you lived on the fat of the land in those places."

"Well, no, you don't actually. But it didn't matter."

Eleanor looked in in a hurry. "Well, *that* was a silly thing to do," she said in the jollying voice she used a great deal with children. "Fancy falling off a roof."

'Her mind is not on what she is saying,' Julia thought. 'She is talking to him like a nursemaid.'

"Tea, Eleanor?" she asked, laying her hands on the warm sides of the teapot.

"No, I must go. Chris Aldridge is waiting for me downstairs."

"Bring him up, then."

"The stairs are difficult for him and it's not worth it, for we are just off to the cinema."

"His time must be nearly up, surely," said Julia. "It is going to be embarrassing for us all if he is going to over-run it."

Eleanor could not view the subject with the same detachment.

"Is nothing sacred to you?" she cried.

"Mr Aldridge certainly isn't," said Julia, lifting the lid of the teapot and looking inside.

But, when Eleanor had gone downstairs, she repented, and leaning out of the window called down to them as they set off and waved cheerfully at Mr Aldridge as if she could overlook his doctor's miscalculations. "Won't you come back to supper?" she shouted. "The Mallorys are coming, Eleanor."

"Oh, then I don't think we will," said Eleanor, who could not change her mood as quickly, nor as often, as Julia.

'Good!' thought Julia, as she gave a last smile and wave and turned away from the window.

"Why are you pleased that Eleanor won't be home to supper?" Oliver asked, his cheeks more than ever hollowed as he sucked his milk up through a straw.

" Don't be absurd," she blustered. " And don't make those disgusting noises with your drink."

He looked at her reproachfully, knowing that the fuss and luxury was over and normality regained. She sensed this as she took the tray from him. "Would you like me to read to you? What shall it be?" she asked. "*Swiss Family* or *The Red House*?" For it was usually one of these he chose when he was ill.

"*Swiss Family*," said Oliver. "The part about the savages."

She fetched the faded, old-fashioned book she had had as a child and began to read.

" The father is really too clever," Oliver interrupted. " It would be better if it was someone else writing the book. The trouble with all these ' I ' books is the boasting. Except *Kidnapped*," he added.

" Do you want to listen or not?"

" Listen."

" I'm not reading this for my own pleasure," Julia lied, tapping the page with her knuckles. "What a very long chapter this is."

At last she came to the end of it. " I think it must be the only one in the book which doesn't end with prayers and going to sleep. It is really rather a sickening story. The more one loves it, the more sickening it becomes. And the way he finds wives for them all, on top of all his other finds, is really the last straw." She yawned, replaced the book-mark, the skeleton of a lime-leaf, and closed the book with reverence.

" It's time to wash me now," said Oliver, " and to take my temperature."

" Oh, God, you are like an old man at Tunbridge Wells," she cried.

When she brought in the bowl of warm water, he rolled

up his sleeves carefully. "Only up to the elbows at night," he explained.

"How long will this routine go on for?" she asked. "Must this house be turned into a hospital? Have I to do everything like an illiterate nurse and talk to children as if they are imbeciles and to grown-ups as if they are children?"

He giggled, dabbing at the very middle of his face with the flannel.

When he had settled down, and she had carried the vases of flowers away as he directed, she went downstairs to get supper. Two tearful nights and the excitement of the day had tired her. She wished that she might go to bed, instead of preparing food for other people.

'It doesn't matter what sort of meal it is,' she decided, smashing eggs recklessly into a bowl, smearing the omelette-pan with garlic. 'I have an excuse for everything that goes wrong.'

Her favourite Corporal had brought the eggs to the back door during the morning. He no longer fixed his gaze upon the plate-rack but brought out photographs of his sister's children and even letters in coloured ink from his fiancée, sought Julia's advice on birthday presents and in return always told her what films to be sure not to miss.

Roddy came home and wandered round the dining-room table, holding glasses to the light to see if they were smeared, and straightening the knives and forks.

'Now, I feel *I* want to be cherished,' Julia was thinking, as she put plates to warm. 'I want someone to bring *me* a three-and-ninepenny peach or a pearl ring in a velvet box . . .' Here the Mallorys arrived—empty-handed.

Mrs Mallory held herself responsible, she said at once, for Oliver's accident. She could not apologise enough: no amount of repetition seemed to satisfy her.

"Not at all," Julia murmured, without thought, as she

ladled rich brown onion soup on to fried bread, offered cheese, sipped . . . with a wry mouth, she glanced at Roddy, wondering what it was she was sipping and if it were turning her teeth black. She tipped it quickly into her soup.

"Felicity was heart-broken," said Mrs Mallory, attributing to her daughter the suitable reaction. "I could do nothing with her the next day, could I, Robert?"

"She is pretty generally unmanageable," he agreed. "This really *is* soup."

"They had become such little pals."

"I hope they still are," said Julia.

"A meal in itself," said the Wing Commander, cracking open a bread roll with a loud report.

Julia fetched in the omelettes and a dish of beans.

"There is something so foreign about your cooking," said Mrs Mallory kindly, not quite knowing what it was—the sensation of garlic in her mouth.

Roddy thought Julia was in a reckless mood. Her cooking endorsed this. 'It is the reaction,' he decided. 'She is over-wrought. If anything should happen to that boy . . .'

"I should like a glass of water, I think," said poor Mrs Mallory, putting her plump hand over her wine-glass.

'Is this meal a failure or a success?' Roddy asked himself, pouring out cold water for Mrs Mallory and watching her husband taking forkfuls of omelette with energy and almost with abandon.

"Felicity is such a tomboy," Mrs Mallory continued, when her thirst was slaked. "As if Oliver's accident were not enough for one week, this morning she must needs climb the greengage tree and get caught up and tear her . . ." she glanced at Roddy and continued in a slightly lower voice . . ." her viyella. She really is a handful. It's a masterpiece."

"Now here come the wasps," said her husband, swishing about with his table-napkin, as Julia brought in a dish of

154

apples. Roddy gave a smart clap now and then with his hands and sometimes a wasp fell more or less stunned to the carpet.

"These baked apples are very good," said the Wing Commander.

"I had the recipe from *Villette*. I like to get my recipes from good literature," Julia explained.

"It takes a woman novelist to describe a dish of food."

"If we invert that, what a prodigious novelist Mrs Beeton would have been," said Roddy.

"Oh, I agree," said Julia, "but it isn't often true. Remember how it is always mutton in Jane Austen. I can't recall them eating anything else. Oh, gruel, of course."

"And don't men describe food well?" Mrs Mallory wondered.

No one could remember. "One of the best meals I ever ate in my imagination was the Boeuf en daube in *To the Lighthouse*," said Julia. "I see it now and smell it—the great earthenware dish and its" (she closed her eyes and breathed slowly) "'its confusion of savoury brown and yellow meats, and its bayleaves and its wine'."

They laughed at her and she took up a spoon and was surprised that the taste was of fruit, not meat.

"Virginia Woolf is a little too modern for me," said the Wing Commander. "She has not stood the test of time. She has not been approved by posterity."

"We have none of us been that," said Julia. "But we can still enjoy a meal."

"Do let us all help wash up," said Mrs Mallory, as if this would be a great lark. She was not surprised, only relieved (for there was her black satin to be considered) when Julia pushed back her chair and, with a look of impatience at the wreckage of the table, said it could be left. "Yes, leave it," she repeated, as if in the meantime someone else

would deal with it. The Mallorys had made similar grand gestures and respected Julia's. It was obvious that when they had gone, Roddy and Julia, tired and bickering slightly, would sigh and groan over all the plates and knives and forks, go up to bed saying ' thank God for that ' and wondering if it was worth it.

" Hush ! " said Julia suddenly, her table-napkin still in her hand. They paused obediently, froze in the middle of their gestures as in a fairy-tale. Roddy, as the host and a man of action, very soon took the lead, striding to the door and opening it.

" Who is Oliver talking to? Or is he delirious ? " cried Julia, and, as a mother, was the first up the stairs.

The Mallorys, as guests, scarcely knew what course to take and thought it best to wait hesitantly in the middle of the hall, wearing expressions of alertness and concern. ' If we can help, we are here,' they seemed to say.

Oliver, the bandage now over his eyes, slept deeply.

" He was talking in his sleep," Roddy explained, yet the explanation would scarcely do, as the conversation all at once recommenced.

" It's that girl," Julia said suddenly. Roddy moved towards the attic stairs, frowning in annoyance.

Downstairs in the hall, Mrs Mallory stood looking up at a picture of a woman with one breast exposed and a goblet in her hand. The Wing Commander, not especially interested in this, wandered back into the dining-room.

" The Lippincote girl," Julia added, but Roddy was already up the stairs. The door of the attic-room was ajar and inside, sitting before a mirror with her face framed in pale marabout, was Miss Lippincote.

" This is going too far," Roddy pointed out, staring at the feathery scarf, which was a deeper colour at the ends as if it had been toasted.

156

She looked at him through the mirror.

"I have no quarrel with your mother," he continued. "But this is inexcusable. How did you enter the house? When did you come?"

Now she turned round from the mirror and slowly unwound the marabout. "I was getting ready to go to a dance," she explained. "Now I shan't go, for you have spoiled it for me."

"Don't talk nonsense," he said loudly.

"It is true. I should never enjoy it now."

"Roddy," said Julia gently, her hand on his arm, her gaze travelling greedily over the room, which she, unlike Oliver, had wanted for so long to see.

The furniture was cheap fretwork stuff with a grain, emphatically but rather pointlessly, painted all over it. A wardrobe door stood open showing a long line of crushed-up party dresses, the colours of sweet-peas and a great deal sequinned. Across the bed and floor was a litter of ribbons and velvet flowers and scarves. A faint, stale, womanly smell pervaded the room.

"Oh, this!" cried Julia, forgetting herself and darting forward.

"That is my mother's wedding dress," said Miss Lippincote with dignity.

"Of course, I recognise it. Champagne lace over cream peau-de-soie." She took a piece of the skirt in her fingers and the silk cracked and split, brittle with age.

"The lace is very old. I should have worn it at my own wedding." She stood up and looked out of the turret-window, fiddling with the little acorn at the end of the blind-cord. "How can I be married from a private hotel?"

"Really, Miss Lippincote!" said Roddy. "I have guests downstairs. I cannot concern myself with your wedding arrangements. Perhaps you will take what you want and

157

we can lock up this room. I shall communicate with your mother in the morning."

'What grand words men use!' Julia reflected, lifting the wedding dress once more to examine the finish of the seams.

Miss Lippincote struck the window-pane with the wooden acorn, sighed and turned away. Her fingers lingered sensitively on the discarded marabout, flicked open an ostrich feather fan and let the curling fronds of it rest on her cheek. Roddy held the door wide and stood there, looking like an officer. Julia hesitated, reluctant to leave the room, with so much detail still to be disclosed. Miss Lippincote put on a fawn raincoat, which had been hanging on the bedpost, and held out her hand to Julia, as if she would rather say goodbye there, on her own territory. She and Roddy held aloof from one another.

"We should prefer it if you would let us know next time you wish to have access to this room," Roddy said, turning the key and handing it to her. "The arrangement, in any case, was with your mother." He followed her sternly down the stairs. "So perhaps you will discuss the matter with her," he continued, for he must have the last word, "and come to a more satisfactory arrangement."

He did not have the last word. "Thank you so much," she cried with sudden archness, when she reached the front door.

"Now, Roddy, what is this?" cried the Wing Commander, coming out into the hall again. "Is there a skeleton in some cupboard? Are you smuggling young women into the house?"

"*Out* of the house, sir," said Roddy.

"It was very rude of us," Julia admitted. "But I have so few adventures and I could not bear to be left out of that one. Although I should have been afraid to go up the stairs on my own."

Roddy was still angry, and he handed round cigarettes in silence.

"I thought you were awfully harsh," Julia told him, to make matters worse. "The poor creature is so obviously . . ."

"That makes me even less anxious to have her drifting in and out."

"The room is like a foreign embassy, a little patch of territory over which we have no authority."

"She will find the privilege about as much use as they do in the diplomatic world," said Roddy grimly.

Julia suddenly discovered she was now less frightened of *Mrs* Lippincote.

"I don't see why," said the Wing Commander. "The very best of families have mad daughters. It never diminishes their importance. Rather increases it."

"All the same, I am not quite so intimidated. Oh, here come Eleanor and Mr Aldridge. Eleanor, we have had such an adventure." She hoped, remembering the wreckage in the dining-room, to put Eleanor in a good mood.

"And how are you keeping, Mr Aldridge?" she asked— a question more suitable for a corpse, she realised. Eleanor flopped into a chair, as if she had every intention of remaining there till bedtime, and waited for the threads of any conversation she may have interrupted to be picked up again for her benefit.

"What about something to eat?" Julia suggested, thinking this might direct her towards the dining-room.

"We've been very vulgar, very low," said Eleanor with an affected laugh. "We have been in a dreadful spit-and-sawdust bar eating sandwiches and drinking ale."

"Very nice, too," said the Wing Commander robustly.

Roddy thought it gentlemanly of him to take it like that, but he was shocked at Eleanor's confessing such things before strangers. It was unlike her. Better Eleanor than Julia,

though, he decided. Eleanor conveyed a feeling of shame, of knowing her behaviour eccentric. Julia wouldn't have done so much.

Mr Aldridge, immune from human condemnation, smiled comfortably at Mrs Mallory, who, like all the rest, was drawn to him immediately by sensations of pity and tenderness.

CHAPTER 18

FELICITY HAD an elephant's trunk of plasticene clamped to the bridge of her nose. She let it rove over the tea-table, until it fell off into the sugar basin. Oliver giggled shrilly, but Julia had become irritable. 'Children have their own jokes,' she decided, 'and they always go on too long.' She was surprised at Oliver. Had this strange sense of humour been there always, needing another child to bring it into play?

"Why do you stare so at Felicity?" he asked her, the giggling ceasing sharply on an indrawn breath.

"I was thinking she is like her father," Julia said carelessly. The sombre nobility of feature, even broken up by merriment, could never be attractive in a girl.

"I have my mother's eyes," she said.

"Look at me."

Beautifully candid, the child's eyes widened. With her waiting gaze fixed still on Julia's face, she fumbled on her plate for her sandwich and took a bite.

"Yes." Julia smiled. "You have your mother's eyes."

"Here comes a lady up the drive," said Oliver, who faced the window.

"Oh, God!" Julia cried, putting a hand on her bosom, like a woman in a play. "It's Mrs Lippincote."

"She has changed her hat, then," said Oliver. "I don't like this one so well."

"Children, come away from the window!"

Julia searched under her chair for hair-pins, thrust a couple into the toppling fronds at the nape of her neck, saw crumbs all over the carpet, and found herself hissing at the children:

"Stay quietly in this room and don't come out until I tell you."

She rushed to the drawing-room as the door-bell rang and had time only to retrieve the photograph of Mrs Lippincote in court feathers from the bureau-drawer and prop it up in its original place.

She crossed the hall at a casual pace, and with a look of hostility, which she imagined was an air of self-possession, opened the door.

"I am Mrs Lippincote."

Superfluous statement.

The leghorn hat with its immense velvet bow, the tussore suit and parasol, the gold chains and watch pinned to the bosom, transfixed Julia. The bosom itself intimidated, seemed unrelated to the female body, a structure, a shelf, a thing to pin watches to, hang chains upon.

"How do you do." Julia held back the door and stretched her lips in welcome. Accompanying Mrs Lippincote across her own hall, she heard (but could discover no means of stopping) her own insincerities, one after another: pleasure at meeting, gratitude for benefits conferred, humility at living in Mrs Lippincote's house. Recklessly she admired and condoled, apologised for the war and felt able to promise better things for the future.

Mrs Lippincote sat beside the empty grate and looked at

her. Her eyes, refusing to travel the room, avoiding the vulgarity of noting alterations or making comparisons, were levelled too attentively at Julia, who thought: '*My* eyes would have been everywhere and betrayed me. *She* has been trained not to betray herself.' She suddenly had no more to say. There was a little silence and then Mrs Lippincote took a small piece of paper from her tapestry handbag and glanced at it quickly. "Firstly, the coal," she began. "I am afraid I overlooked that point in my discussion with your husband. Before the summer is over will you please replace what you have used. I should like the stock kept up."

"Oh, it is done," said Julia eagerly. It was like an oral examination—alternating doubt and relief and the strain too great to be borne for any length of time. "We are full to overflowing," she added.

"If you are going with the end of summer drawing near, it might be impossible to replenish."

"We *are* replenished. We couldn't be more so. And there is no likelihood of our going."

"Oh."

"No. None at all."

"Well, then . . . now Mrs Whapshott. She is working satisfactorily for you?"

"Quite," said Julia fervently.

"I hear she has changed her day to Monday."

"Yes."

"I thought it a pity."

"It was her own idea, and one day is as good as another to me."

After this outrageous admission, there was a brief pause.

"Anyone following you here as a tenant might find it an awkward day—Monday," Mrs Lippincote resumed.

"Perhaps no one *will* follow us. Perhaps we shall be here until the end of the war, until you come back yourself. Then

there will be women for everyone and everyday," she added, madly optimistic as well as ambiguous.

"You are not thinking of leaving, then?"

"Why, no!"

"Then my nephew, Desmond Maffick, informed me wrongly."

"I can't think why . . ."

"Oh, it is a common failing in him. He is all rush and humbug and very prone to summing up a situation before it has taken place. I am afraid my poor sister spoilt him. He was an only child."

Julia flushed.

"And then entering the Church has only furthered the mischief. So many women and too many afternoon calls— a life, one is sad to say, of gossip and paltry intrigue. I must apologise for his mistake. The next thing, the last thing, is this!" She opened her gloved hand and offered a key to Julia.

"It is the key of the little attic room. It was a kind suggestion of your husband's, but not really necessary, and it has led, I'm afraid, to misunderstandings. I would rather you had it," she insisted, as Julia demurred. Her jaw-line tightened and, for the first time, she glanced round the room. "I believe you have been inconvenienced. My daughter did not quite understand. She has . . ." now even her glance faltered . . . "She has . . . difficulties," she ended primly.

"Would you like a cup of tea?" asked Julia, who had enough breeding to know that at all emergencies—birth, death or defeat—cups of tea must at once be offered.

"It is rather late," Mrs Lippincote murmured, lifting her watch.

"There is some practically freshly made," said Julia confidently. "I was having tea late, with the children."

" Children ? "

" Oliver and his little friend."

Once Julia had gone, Mrs Lippincote's restraint went too. Her eyes, like fish in a tank, went to each wall, to every corner, dived to the darkness beneath the sofa, vaguely discerned the warming-pan lying there, and returned to the surface, as it were, every time she heard a movement in the house, a footstep, or the clink of crockery. She tried to analyse—and dislike—the difference in the room and could do neither. What had been a colour scheme was broken up. A dark red cushion from the dining-room and an emerald green one from upstairs lay on the pink sofa. Sunflowers (in the drawing-room!) and scarlet carnations were arranged in the same vase. Mrs Lippincote shifted uneasily, but warily in her chair.

Julia found Oliver and Felicity eating peacefully.

" Is she cross with you ? " Oliver whispered.

" Cross? Of course not." Julia was often appalled at how little she could conceal from him.

' Perhaps it will worry her if she thinks we are using good china for every day,' she thought, selecting two breakfast-cups with blue bands, and filling them with tea, which was certainly not fresh and scarcely warm. She hissed more exhortations and threats at the children and left them drinking their milk out of heavily rivetted Crown Derby cups.

" I should like to meet your little boy," said Mrs Lippincote, having sipped her tea and crumbled a soft biscuit into the saucer.

" He will be in in a moment, when they have finished eating," Julia said, striving to appear a fond and placid mother. She saw Eleanor passing the window outside with Miss Cowper. She was looking inquiringly at the figure seated with its back to her, making little questioning gestures

164

which merely confused Julia, who could only look out of the window without any expression at all.

"You are company for one another," said Mrs Lippincote when Eleanor was introduced. "It must be a pleasant arrangement, living together."

"Yes," they both agreed at once. Julia was conscious of a wave of sweat breaking out over her body, from the anguish of the last quarter-of-an-hour.

Miss Cowper's long white fingers twisted vaguely in the roll of hair on her shoulders.

"Eleanor, *would* you like to ask Oliver and Felicity to come in, if they have finished their tea?"

They awaited the children in silence but with confidence and enthusiasm, as Lady Hester Stanhope is said to have awaited the Messiah.

Oliver certainly sensed this, the fact that he and Felicity had been brought in to ease the situation and create a diversion.

"This is Oliver. Oliver, say how-do-you-do to Mrs Lippincote."

"How-do-you-do."

"And how old are you, Oliver?"

"I am seven, but backward for my age."

"Oh, I am sure that is not so. Once I had three little boys like you. And now the younger, the baby, is a Major in India!"

"Are you Whig or Jacobite?" Oliver asked, withdrawing his hand from hers.

"And this is Felicity Mallory," Julia said quickly.

Felicity came forward reluctantly. She would not put out her hand and ducked slightly when her head was being patted.

"*Un peu gavroche*," muttered Miss Cowper, leaning back negligently against the bureau, her hands thrust into her

pockets, her shoulders hunched up, for she did not care, she was happy to think, a twopenny cuss either way for Mrs Lippincote or for Julia.

CHAPTER 19

ON SUNDAY MORNINGS in Vasco Street, nobody got up early, except Leo to make tea. Eleanor, who was supposed to be sleeping at Sunnybank, would have liked to rise, for she was not really comfortable lying on the sofa under Sarge's leather coat; but she was afraid of disturbing the others and could think of nothing to do anyway.

The light seems to have a different quality on Sunday mornings; a rather cold hard light lay over the walls of that little front sitting-room, which never came to life unless full of people late at night and softened by a haze of smoke.

Down below in the street a few people went along the pavement, perhaps home from Church or from fire-watching. It was a staccato beat on the early morning pavements, the sound thrown up from great depths and echoing as on the steep sides of a well.

She shifted and the leather coat, creaking, slid from her as it had done all night. 'With the winter coming,' she thought, 'I shall be cold here at night.'

Then Leo tapped on the door and carried in the cup of tea and a bowl of sugar. Not a drop spilt into the saucer, she observed, sitting up and smiling. She made no gesture of covering her bosom, as she always would before Roddy. It was as if Leo, voiceless, was therefore to her less than a man.

166

He closed the door and, going along the dark passage, thought: 'There is only one kind of tact that's any use. And that's the tact that precedes one; no, pre*vents* one. Goes before. The tact of a person with so much finer an imagination than oneself that the risk one has run is never discovered. And the one who is capable of being tactful in such a way is the only one who has also the secret of complete cruelty.'

Vera sat up in bed, her bare shoulders looking polished. She yawned and took up a great bunch of her navy-blue hair and thrust it back from her forehead. As she did so, he could see the darker, apricot-coloured skin below her armpit.

Sarge would not wake. He lay there, puffing a little through his lips, sometimes whistling faintly like a far-off train. A stern line curved from his nose to mouth.

"When he is asleep, he is a Roman Emperor," she said. She smacked him and he merely rolled away from her, towards the edge of the bed. She laughed at Leo and put the tea on a chair beside her. Then she stretched her arm and felt on the floor for the book she had dropped there the last thing the night before and began to read.

Then Leo took two cups into Kirsty's room. She still slept, her body curled round under the bedclothes, legs drawn up like an unborn creature in the womb. The room was darkened, untidy. He put down the tray and began to gather up her clothes from the floor. Carelessness about belongings distressed him. He was affronted by it everywhere in the house.

Neatness was a mania with him. He must even straighten pairs of shoes—he did so now—and have brushes placed symmetrically on dressing-tables and pots of cream lined up in diminishing heights like soldiers. Her brassiere still had the shape of her breasts, the shoulder-straps had

curled into a thin grubby string; her knickers were flecked with blood. He loved her beyond being fastidious.

When he had cleared the floor, he went over to the bed and held the cup of tea close to her face. The steam of it, the aroma, made her nose quiver like a sleeping cat's. She awoke and stared at him. "I'll tell you what I was dreaming," she said at once. "Quick! Listen, before I forget!"

She laced her fingers into his. "I was painting a picture. It was called 'Making Pyjamas'. Oh, let me just keep it, while I describe it to you." She narrowed her eyes and then closed them. "There was a woman sitting at a sewing-machine with a black line round her, like Matisse. Out of the sewing-machine billowed yards and yards of striped stuff like ectoplasm coming out of a medium's mouth." She giggled. "In front of the fire, a man was trying on a pyjama-jacket. He was looking into the mirror and buttoning it up. It only reached to his bottom—a bad place for it to end really." She ducked into the bedclothes with her giggles. "The front of his legs," she at length continued, "were hairy and rosy from the fire. The backs a sort of bluish-white with veins. On the mantelpiece there was a green marble clock and a bunch of pampas-grass. You think I am making it up as I go along, but I'm not. I've never seen a naked man, not even *half*-naked—well, not *that* half— and to think my first glimpse should be so . . . Was *I* the woman at the sewing-machine?"

He looked at her consideringly.

"You are trying to remember what Freud and those chaps would say."

He nodded and began to drink his tea. She shifted on to one elbow and sipped her own. "There must be something in me," she continued, "for me to get such dreams. Well, they almost amount to visions. I don't see why you laugh. I have never heard of anyone else who had dreams in the least

like mine. Never. Look at that one where I was climbing on the roof of that church. You just look smug like that to make out it meant something shameful. Everyone does that nowadays and nothing aggravates me more. Oh, Leo, why can't we be married? I have so set my heart on it. I know you would never regret it, if only you would. Or if we could try it and if you didn't like it, I'd always go off and leave you in peace; I do, honestly promise that. Let me go in now and tell Sarge we're going to. He would never let us *not* be married." He shook his head and holding the palm of her hand to his lips put little kisses into it.

"If we were married," she went on, "and I could make you peaceful, and I know I could—oh, I know you appear more peaceful than me, but you aren't really, inside—well, then, it may all come back to you and you'll be better and then there could never be anything more to worry us until the end of our days."

She tipped her cup over the saucer and then looked at the tea leaves. "It's a fine thing for a Marxist to say," she added, "but I do see signs of happiness here." She cheated, though, moving one tea leaf alongside another to improve the omens.

.

'With the winter coming on,' thought Eleanor, sitting up, 'I shall have to come to some decision. Or if the war should end, that would force the issue, too.' The awful thing about life is only having *one*. And not being able to keep your cake and eat it. Such a little thing to ask, and so reasonable. Roddy, she knew, would never countenance her coming here, and how much longer she could continue to take advantage of his lack of interest in her, she did not know. Besides Roddy, there was her job. How could she be sure that Sarge would not ask her to do things which might lose her her job—

for instance, selling the *Daily Worker* outside Woolworths, which they so often discussed doing. Or marching—she trembled—in a procession.

And yet her instinct, her inclination, she decided, getting up at last and discarding Sarge's coat, led her to believe that *here* was her place, here the centre of her existence, among those who accepted her (as Julia never had) and treated her with courtesy; perhaps love, too, she thought, perhaps love and kindness and companionship.

At last Sarge woke up. The exquisite relief of Sunday morning was like slipping into a deep hot bath. He lay and stretched in the luxury of it.

"There's your Branch meeting at eleven-thirty," said Vera, handing him his tea. "Leo did the circular letters. You could take some with you to the Trades Council this afternoon."

"Yes, that's right." He yawned and sat up, for the bath-water, like the tea (he grimaced) seemed to have turned chilly.

"It was absurd," she added, "to let the open-air meeting clash with the women's meeting. That sort of thing is one of our chief failures."

"Our chief failure is that there are only seven nights in the week," he told her, handing back his empty cup. "We have always found that frustrated us. If you could nurse Eleanor along, she might be very useful to you—perhaps take on the women's group altogether and free you for your classes."

"Eleanor?"

"Why not? She could at least take charge of a meeting, if you drew up the agenda with her beforehand. Who else

have you got who can do that? Mrs Thomas? Hilda? Norah? Kirsty's too scatter-brained."

"Eleanor will never be any good."

"Hush!"

"I'm not shouting."

"No, but one's own name always seems to carry miles. Why do you feel like that about her?"

"Oh, these middle-class women take up one thing after another. It'll be spiritualism next month and cosmo-therapy or whatever it is the month after, and as like as not, pacifism and the Hay diet before *this*. She's bored and lonely, that's all."

"She admits as much. She's dissatisfied with life as it is and wants it different. What better motive have *you*?"

"Nothing personal. You know that."

"Then you're a marvel."

"I see disease that has to be carved away. Men don't become surgeons merely to satisfy their love of cutting up."

"Don't they? Well, as I say, you're a marvel. But you can't disqualify all the other chaps who aren't marvels, who've got personal motives, poor devils, and can't be side-tracked. Chaps like me even. What I went through when I was young, what I saw my mother suffer, makes it impossible for me ever to have the surgeon's view. I'm much more like the man under the knife. I am quite sincere, though," he assured her, committing himself once more to the luxury of the warm, heavy bed-clothes.

"Well"—she snapped up her book. "You'll see! We've known a few and I'll bet she's no different from the rest. After a bit, they drop off. As soon as they get scared. Look at Finland! It seems like taking it easy in a gilded coach at the moment, but things may change, and then you'll see."

He drew her elbow away from under her and she dropped down beside him.

" Darling ! "

" Yes, Sarge ? "

" Just shut up, will you ? "

She began to answer back and then it all seemed useless and instead she raised her arms and slid down close to him, gathering up her long hair with one hand deftly, and tucking it away under her head.

CHAPTER 20

" ARE YOU making a bid for my soul ? " Julia asked Mr Maffick. She was swatting flies, one hand to her breast, the folded telephone directory in the other.

He sighed. " Women really think that there is God on one side and the devil on the other, duelling for their souls. It is flattering to them, no doubt."

" I think you are being rather rude. Anyhow that's what religion is, surely ? It teaches us about the tussle between good and evil. Doesn't it ? "

" Perhaps we can grant you that you have a very rough idea of it all," he said, with a smile which, if it was not mysterious, was certainly prim.

" Anyway, I said ' you ', not ' God '." She resumed her swatting in a wild, ferocious way, which was better at least for the flies.

" I really don't care twopence for your soul."

" Well, then, you should. It is your job. You are being paid to save me and you really should put up some sort of a fight. Isn't it awful, this stroking movement flies do with their front legs ? I know a Roman Catholic priest—Father Arnold—and he put up a better show than you."

172

" What did he do? "

" He lent me a lot of books about how awful it is in Russia."

" Was that fighting for your soul? "

" I thought it was a beginning."

" Why did you wait for those two to get away? "

" I never hit them when they're copulating. It would be simply the limit. Would *you* like that? " she asked with a show of innocence.

" Well, I should dislike being hit anyway. Whether I was " —he swallowed—" copulating or not would make so little difference." His face shone with tolerance and daring.

" Surely there are more flies than when I started? "

They seemed to be circling low over the whole room. She felt them crawling on her face, in a leisurely way, as if she were a corpse.

" They say that when you kill a fly, two more come to its funeral."

" That's what they're doing, then."

" What about fly-papers? "

" No, they're so cruel. Imagine it! Striving to free oneself until the legs leave the sockets. This way is bad enough. Contemplating brutality makes you used to it. It's a way of saving our reason—of putting armour over one's nerves. If I really imagined what I'm doing now, I couldn't do it. It is the first step towards committing atrocities on human beings. At first, you are nervously repelled, then take it for granted, then look to it for excitement and, finally, for pleasure and ecstasy. Then you're done for and must be shot. Actually, you're done for by the time you've got half-way up the ladder. I'm on the bottom rung."

" Do you intend to jump down, or proceed? "

" I think I am going on up, willy-nilly. This morning I read in the paper about something vile the Nazis did, and I

thought: 'It's all right. It's not as bad as the atrocity I read about last week.' I was very much shocked at myself."

"War does that for one."

"Yes. That's what I said. The contemplation of brutality brutalises. Last time, you didn't get your tea. This time you shall have it." She laid down the blood-stained directory and went to put the kettle on. When she had gone, he sat still for a moment and then began cautiously to tiptoe round the room.

On the table was a copy of *The Tenant of Wildfell Hall* with a greasy paper d'oyley in it as a book-mark. On the mantelpiece was propped a card with '*Kriegsgefangenenlager*' printed on it, and a few lines of writing in indelible pencil—"Keeping quite fit. Few games of Footer. Not heard lately. Mail irregular. See you soon. All the best." 'Just the sort of letter one likes to get,' he thought sarcastically. The mantelpiece clock whirred and struck, making him start guiltily.

There were the unnerving sounds of children entering the house. 'It will be dining-room tea, then,' he thought in annoyance, picturing from his experience and without enthusiasm, the hostess inattentive, full of little warnings and exhortations to the children, with scarcely half a mind for the visitor, who is expected—as a visitor, and still more as a clergyman—to look upon the children with love and geniality.

Julia had begun her admonitions already in the kitchen, starting with the usual one about wiping feet on the mat. "And, Oliver, no impertinent questions about politics or religion. And no giggling. And give Bonnie Prince Charlie a rest for once."

"Yes, mother."

"And carry this jug of milk in."

"Yes,"

"And don't slop it."

"No, mother."

"Felicity"—quite a different manner and tone of voice—"I wonder would you be awfully kind and carry the jam in for me?"

"Yes, Mrs Davenant."

In a little procession they made their way to the dining-room.

"Tea is ready," said Julia, appearing at the drawing-room door with a tea-cosy in her hand. Mr Maffick sat in his chair just as she had left him.

"Ah, the children!" he cried, beaming magnificently upon them as they sat, now more or less subdued, on either side of the table. "I used to have tea at this very table when I was a little boy."

They stared, not able to comprehend the suggestion behind this piece of information.

"They can't believe I ever *was* a little boy," he said with a light laugh. "What have you been doing all the after-noon?"

"Sweating," said Felicity.

Oliver, with a quick look at his mother, said:

"We went to watch the Squadron Sports and then we practised jumping."

"Corporal Crook won the long jump," said Felicity.

"He comes often to this house," Oliver boasted.

"He doesn't go short of much," quoted Felicity.

"*L'enfant terrible sera terrible,*" said Mr Maffick in parents' French.

"That is a nasty cough you have, Felicity," said Julia.

"I have always been a bit chesty."

Oliver waved his hands over the cakes and a few flies scattered.

"Well, September is nearly here," said Mr Maffick,

" Oliver will be starting at Sunny Bank, and what about Felicity? "

A little shadow of dread darkened her eyes.

" Felicity is coming almost next door," said Julia, who noted the shadow. " She will be running in and out to see us often."

But Felicity's eyes were fixed on Oliver's as if only in his could she see a true reflection or any hope at all.

" Who is reading *The Tenant of Wildfell Hall*? " Mr Maffick inquired.

" I am," Julia admitted, cutting a slab of gingerbread into oblongs and offering some to Felicity, who shook her head.

" Oh, come! I made it especially for you, with dates, because I know you like dates."

But Felicity's appetite was gone. " It *is* very nice, but I don't like it much," she said in a little croaking voice.

" *Un peu distraite*," said Mr Maffick. " I will take some if I may. I remember that book well—a fairly haunting study of disintegration, *n'est ce pas*? "

" If you have finished your milk, Oliver, you and Felicity may be excused," said Julia. The children gulped at their beakers and scrambled down. " Yes, disintegration," she murmured, slipping a hand inside the tea-cosy for warmth and turning her attention to him at last. " I suppose she had first-hand experience of *that*."

" What a life of darkness and frustration! "

They contemplated in silence their separate pictures of Haworth Parsonage with sleet falling over the tombstones.

" Lucky for us Emily was not a man," said Julia, " or *she* might have drunk herself to death at the Black Bull. It was better to write *Wuthering Heights*, but she really had no choice. Men are not forced to turn their desolation to advantage as women are. It's easier for them to dissipate their

passion, quell their restlessness in other ways. The Brontë girls just couldn't slip down to the pub. So they had to take to writing. What is it, Oliver?"

"Corporal Crook came with this letter."

"Has he gone?"

"No, he's just showing his vaccination to Felicity."

"Will you ask him if he'd like a cup of tea?"

She murmured conventionally at Mr Maffick and tore open the envelope.

> "*My dearest Julia,*
>
> *Don't keep supper for me as there is a new intake and I may be late.*
>
> *Love, sweetheart.*
>
> RODDY."

"So you are a Brontëphil, too," she resumed, tucking the letter under her plate. "That sounds like a prehistoric animal. What is it now?"

"He *would* like some," said Oliver.

"Oh, yes." She poured out a cup and propped up a piece of gingerbread in the saucer. "Will you ask him to excuse me, but I have visitors."

Oliver was wondering at the unnecessary plural as he went carefully along the passage, carrying the cup of tea.

Corporal Crook had a picture of Christ Crucified tattooed on the inside of his arm. Felicity watched with horrified fascination as he flexed his muscle.

"There is a clergyman in there with my mother," said Oliver.

"That's all right, son. The Padre and me get on O.K." He rolled down his shirt-sleeve and drank his tea.

"He isn't a padre, he's a clergyman," said Felicity.

"Are you a Roman Catholic?" Oliver asked.

"Christ, no, boy. I can't say I believe in God at all."

"You will regret those words one day," said Felicity.

"Why do you say 'Christ' then, if you don't believe in God?"

"Well, son, there you've got me. I didn't use the word in any religious sense—just one of those words you let drop casual, like . . ." He hesitated, and finished his tea instead of continuing.

"Like what?" Felicity insisted.

"Ah, now, then, give me a chance. You'll get a strip torn off me with your questions."

"I suppose you meant 'bloody'," said Felicity, with an air of sophistication and disillusionment.

This amused him and would, he hoped, amuse the others in the guard-room when he returned.

"Now I must push off."

"My mother said excuse her but she has visitors," Oliver explained.

"That's all right. I'll be round again in the morning with a coupla marrows."

"We have plenty of marrows," said Oliver grandly. "We could give *you* some."

"What should I do with a marrow?" he asked, buckling up his belt and then raising a hand, like a policeman. "Now don't tell me. Don't tell me. Thank you for the tea."

He saluted with a rather hollowed palm and clanked away down the stone path.

"I bet he feathers *his* nest," said Felicity. "I wouldn't put anything past one of those N.C.O.'s at 2 Squadron."

Mr Maffick was thinking he must go.

"Time for Benediction, I suppose," Julia said carelessly, trying to speed him out of the house.

"Father Arnold certainly made some headway," he said, as he bade her goodbye.

178

When he had gone, Julia re-read Roddy's note, tore it in half and began to clear the table in tremendous haste.

CHAPTER 21

ELEANOR WAS NOT the only one who went furtively down the Vasco Road, but to Julia it was no ladder to heaven, only a very dreary road full of dirty shops, leading to the river.

Having sped Mr Maffick on his way, swept the tea-things from the table, left Oliver and Felicity to Eleanor as soon as she entered the house, Julia now walked along the road, not, in spite of all her haste, very anxious to reach the end of her walk, sad as she supposed it would be—Mr Taylor ill, peevish, drunk, hopelessly awaiting his sister (who was always coming to-morrow) in that bungalow, which, each visit, was a little filthier.

The decision that she could not tell Roddy of these visits seemed (Roddy would have condemned her as fanciful) the crucial point of their marriage, forcing her, as it did at last, to see that there was no longer any room in his heart for the weak or unsuccessful, that it was necessary even to shield them from his contempt or condescension.

These thoughts (the road, she noticed, ran and swam with gold, bicycle wheels going slowly through it were covered with a rich patina) were nothing strange to her. During the last few years, unnoticed, they had come and lain down within her. They were at home with her, part of her, to the extent that it seemed now that the knowledge of them flowed with her blood, lay behind her eyes and controlled her vision, heard every movement of her heart.

179

Even coming to such momentous conclusions, saying out
loud as it were, what she had kept silent about before, it was
still in her nature to find other people irresistible. She could
not restrain herself from going lingeringly by those couples
of women who stand always by the windows of shops. She
could even look at shelves of dummy cartons and fly-blown
showcards and listen at ease.

" Even if he gets an artificial leg it's not like a real one."

" No," the other woman agreed. " That's what Norman
said. ' I don't want to be an officer,' he said. ' I just want
to go home.' "

" And then, with a bike it puts it out of the question.
That'll be the worst thing for him."

' We all have our troubles, then,' thought Julia. ' What a
mummy's boy Norman sounds.'

Shopkeepers were rolling back shutters, drawing blinds.
Every other shop seemed to be a butcher's. Flies gathered
over shallow trays of blood, dotted the tripe folded up like
blankets. ' But here,' she thought, ' is the very king of
butcher's shops.' It was a welter of reds—the brown-red of
the blood, the deep red of beef and the paler red of mutton,
the bluish red of a bunch of carnations in a jam-jar, a rosette
of scarlet between a pig's ears. She looked at the pallid,
lecherous dead face, posed there with its rosette, the folds of
flesh drawn into a sneer, the suggestion that it caricatured
humanity. But behind it and all round, the shop flashed and
swam with garnet, with ruby and amber. The butcher, florid
too and in a bloody apron, came and unhooked the side of
a sheep and put up a sheaf of paper instead. He gave Julia
a brief look as he did so, and she walked on.

She tried to remember Mr Taylor in his former magnifi-
cence in Frith Street, standing, with a fine linen handkerchief
in his cuff, by the little glass house where Louise sat among
her bills and piles of silver. He seldom spoke to the waiters

and never looked at them, but Julia, the merciless observer, noticed always with delight the rapid, furious orders which came somehow from his closed lips when any hitch occurred. She had guessed he was hysterical and petulant, even when he so evenly, so blandly moved forward with his cigarette-lighter to a favoured customer, with the correct blend of deference and contempt. She could not accept Roddy's conjecture that he kissed the little olive-skinned wine waiter, but could imagine that he slapped his face, dismissed and forgave him, a dozen times a week.

These thoughts had accompanied her as far as the river, where a strange inversion had taken place, the river lying solid and oily and the pinkish Italianate buildings on the bank appearing airy and fluid. Beyond the buildings lay the fields of blonde stubble and the dark oval shapes of elms.

She crossed the bridge into the Abbey ruins. She noticed for the first time in a corner a large fig-tree with glossy leaves and a few small green figs. It was penned in by railings as if it had no place, with all its pagan associations, in the monastery dormitory where it grew. 'After all, it is not the Parthenon,' Julia thought, looking up at the unripe figs.

They reminded her of her mother, a tranquil and sluttish woman always to be found eating figs and medlars out of damp paper bags and reading Sophocles. 'On an evening like this,' Julia thought—and tears suddenly pricked her eyes—'she would be sitting in the porch with her book and her steel spectacles and a bottle of cheap claret. When it grew chilly she would take off her spectacles and put them in the book to mark her place, then she would wrap her black chenille shawl round her shoulders and tucking the empty bottle under her arm, come inside, where I should be sitting in a circle of lamplight (oh, God, the smell of the wick when it is first lit!), knocking down moths with my book.' Her coming in on those summer evenings was the signal for bed,

for the last crust covered deeply with butter, and the creaking upstairs to dark bedrooms smelling of apples. 'The peace and simplicity,' she thought, moving away at last from the fig-tree. 'We are a reading, drinking family, and a weeping family,' she thought, blowing her nose and running a knuckle under her eyelid.

'And now for Mr Taylor! What is he coming to?' she wondered, going up the path to the bungalow and staring at a collection of dirty milk bottles by the front door. Surely his sister had not arrived at last, for footsteps, not his, she thought, drew near.

The door was opened by a shapeless mountain of a woman with blonde, greying hair and her great bulk swathed in knitted garments in a confusion of sombre colours.

"Yes, what do you want?"

"I came to see Mr Taylor."

The mouth sank into the folds of colourless flesh, the lips tightened until they disappeared.

"He's gone. He's dead."

Julia saw then that the face was a monstrous caricature of his.

"Are you his mother?"

"Who are you?"

"I was a friend of his in London."

"Oh, London . . . he didn't seem to have many *here*." Her bloodshot eyes surveyed, as if with scorn and detestation, the pleasant river scene beyond the garden. "He died this morning . . . one of his attacks. The char found him."

"I *am* so sorry. Was his sister here?"

"His sister?" A very dangerous, wary look came into the eyes now. "No, she was not here and I can't think why you should think she was. Yes, I'm his mother. We come in at the beginning and the end. The rest of the time they're too grand for us."

Her glance swept over Julia. "Well, us standing here. Come in, why don't you?"

Julia stared down at the row of milk bottles and drove her nails into her palms. "No, I must go. I can't say anything. I am so sorry."

"There's nothing to be afraid of."

Julia felt she was being obscenely teased.

"So you knew him in London."

She tried to lift her eyes.

"When he was manager at the Charlotte? He did well for himself. I used to try to remember that. 'He's done well for himself,' I used to say. If you come in, we could sit in the kitchen."

Julia shook her head.

"Needn't go in *there*, if you don't want to." The voice was dangerous again, the eyes so penetrating that sweat broke out in the small of Julia's back. She felt herself hypnotised almost and 'once I'm in there, I'm done for,' she thought in a panic. 'But she can't *make* me!'

"No," she said loudly. "There's no point in my staying. I'm very sorry and I wish I had come sooner, but I couldn't help that. I'm glad you were here, and goodbye." She raised her eyes at last and saw nothing but grief on the other's face. The mouth twitched, but the lips remained closed. The woman merely shook her head slowly and moved back reluctantly into the hall as Julia turned away.

She walked quickly, with a sensation as if snakes threatened her ankles and every tree or piece of railing had arms ready to restrain her. Through the ruins she went, ran almost over the bridge. Here, on the other side of a stretch of water, she could allow herself to pause. Mist was coming up from the far-off meadows and she noticed that time had passed.

Once more she found herself in the Vasco Road. Pubs

were busy and noisy. 'No Beer' or 'Sold Out' was pencilled on cards in the windows of others. A beautiful girl with long black hair came out of a grocer's shop and hurried along the pavement. It was like a drink of cold water to see someone beautiful, walking so quickly and lightly, so alien to death and disintegration.

Julia stopped by a café where soldiers stood by a counter drinking tea from an urn. She went in. The peculiarly sour smell of khaki nauseated her, and she went through to the back of the shop where there were one or two green-tiled tables and some imitation wisteria in thin vases.

She sat down and stared at the smeared tiles. After a while she realised that no one would be likely to come to her, that she must fetch her own tea from the counter, that the soldiers, moreover, were staring at her. She pushed back her chair clumsily and went to the counter, gave her order in confusion and selected a yellowish rock-cake covered with swollen burnt currants, and went back to her table, slopping the tea into the saucer, setting it all down with a clatter.

The tea was scalding hot and made opaque by a spoonful of condensed milk.

She saw her mother holding a glass of tea—against the white light, saying "It must be transparent like beer." 'And that will be enough of *her* for one evening,' she decided. But she could find no other thoughts to fill her mind, only memories of a picture Mr Taylor had once sketched out for her of *his* mother—something about beauty surely, for the image of beauty had certainly been smuggled into her mind —something about fragility and wearing a child's shoes. The image of the mountainous, uncontrolled flesh, the ravaged and evil face, the large feet in the broken carpet-slippers— all this lay somewhere between her and the green-tiled table.

She willed other pictures into her mind—Mrs Lippincote in her winged hat as Oliver had described it, the Wing

Commander knitting a sock one evening in the Ante-room, Roddy's pink, innocent face and Oliver asleep with violet shadows under his eyes. No vision would stay with her except the one she tried to be rid of. She pushed some coppers under her saucer and got up. Outside, the sky had darkened. She set off towards home, thinking of physical comforts—the fire in her bedroom, a deep, hot bath, a cup of coffee. ' Those are the things I want now,' she thought. ' I am getting old and I want to be comfortable.'

It was quite dark when she reached home. Eleanor opened the door. She hoped it had been a good film. Roddy had just come in and they were making tea. She was in one of her moods of saintly gaiety and self-sacrifice.

" Good," said Julia. " Oh, Roddy! " she cried, as he came out into the hall. " Oh, Roddy! " She put her face against his shoulder.

" What is it? "

" I'm shivery," she said. " I'm tired and awfully shivery."

" It *has* turned a bit nippy," he agreed. He took her fingers and rubbed them in his hands. " I'll bring you a drink to bed. Go and have a hot bath."

" You know everything. All that is what I most want."

" And a hot water bottle, too," he shouted after her, as she was trailing upstairs. As she reached the turn of the stairs she looked down and smiled and he grinned back at her before he went out to the kitchen. She was glad suddenly that his face *was* so pink and innocent. Nothing could have comforted her more.

.

The hot water eased away her tiredness, drew out, she thought, wondering if she were physiologically accurate, the kinks and twists and knots in her muscles and nerves. She

lay in the greenish water, turning on the hot tap with her toes from time to time, her eyes half closed, watching sheets of steam slowly veiling the mirrors.

'Oh, death!' she thought, looking down the length of her body. 'For this—so familiar, so reassuring to me, to become familiar and reassuring no longer, to be destroyed!' Cheerless thoughts assailed her. 'I will be destroyed *quickly*,' she decided. 'Not slowly rotting, turning to dust. God don't let me think of it! Cremation. That's better. It's easier for one's friends to contemplate. Over quicker. A simple service and no prayers. A Bach Chorale, perhaps, and some poetry read out—a Chorus from the *Antigone*—'Πολλὰ τα ϛεινα' and so on, and a passage from Ecclesiastes.' She saw Roddy standing there with Eleanor and Oliver and, strangely, also herself ... Tears stung her eyes. She felt anxiety, too, thinking that a scratchy gramophone needle, wrong timing with the Greek, would render her funeral bathetic. 'But this,' she thought, meaning her body, 'is reality itself to me. I could not believe in it ever not *being*. That I, too . . .' She lifted her hand, pink and crinkled from the hot water, and stared at the palm, at the pattern of one line running across another. 'The girdle of Venus, broken in the middle.' She folded a finger, bent a knuckle, so that she could count her issue. It was indicated in some crease or other. 'Four children.' And then that little cut from opening a tin of baked beans, a white scar she had had for years—she forgot why—and a mole. The line of heart branched in all directions, the line of intellect pitched steeply down. The life-line—it had worried her before, though she believed, she vowed, not a word of it—was very short and ended in a little tassel, a sign, she had been told, of sudden death. Perhaps drowning, she suggested to herself, stretching in the water, moving so that first one breast then the other formed an island, then fetched up from the sea a little hillock of belly and a sloping

piece of thigh. She tried to remember how to plot such contours on a graph, wondered what a cross-section of her thigh would look like, examined a birthmark. A strawberry. It *could* be a strawberry. Her mother, it was true, had eaten strawberries at the picnic when the pony had shied and bolted. It was true also that at the time Julia was at some stage of her journey to life. " Seven months gone," the nurse had said. " That would account for it." " But it was not *one* strawberry," Julia's mother (a more sceptical woman than her daughter) had objected. " Not *one,* but pounds and pounds I'd eaten." ' I ought to be covered with them,' Julia thought, submerging her thigh which had dried and was cold. ' Patterned all over with a design of strawberries.' As she moved the water in the small of her back felt cool. She summoned her will-power and got out, dried herself in an impatient way and went into the bedroom. Roddy had lit the fire and came in with a glass of milk.

" Oh, I'm warmer now—I'm a much nicer person now I'm warm."

" Your neck is still dirty, Julia. It is incredible how you can lie in a bath all that time and come out with a grey neck."

" I always hope it will soak clean."

She gathered the skin from the top of the milk and flicked it into the saucer.

" What film did you see ? "

" I didn't go to the cinema. I didn't ever say I was going."

" Oh, I misunderstood Eleanor."

" That *would* be possible."

He began to walk about the room, as if waiting for something. She knew he was about to fail her—or rather, himself. She said : " I went to see Mr Taylor, but he was dead."

He was looking at himself in the mirror. He had a brush in his hand. His rosy face crumpled like a baby's.

' Oh, dear, all the stages we must now go through,' she

187

thought with cynical detachment. 'We haven't even begun
yet—incredulity, dismay, terror, anger, indignation, self-pity.
Perhaps curiosity and sarcasm wedged in also.' The sight of
his face in the mirror only convinced her of what she knew
already, that in all her crises his help would be denied her,
because he could not become Julia, he could only be himself.
'In the mirror,' she thought, 'he sees something unreal—he
sees the opinion of the world, is driven by fear of the world
and judges me by the world's standards. But the world isn't
real. It has no existence. Mr Taylor is real—or was until
this morning—and I am real, but what is Roddy? He is
just a man looking into a mirror watching his own face
growing angrier.'

He had been talking for a long time, asking questions; she
had even answered some.

"Sordid," he said again and again. "Unnecessary.
Gossip. Furtive."

"Yes, furtive!" she cried. "That is what I can forgive
you least of all."

"*You* forgive *me*?"

"A hypocrite always breeds a dozen more. That's the
nuisance of it."

He brushed his hair until ribbons of light ran over it in
all directions. Then he put the brush down and smiled.

'He has run the whole gamut of human emotions, as they
say in the local papers,' she decided. She sipped her milk,
but her thoughts did not match the innocence of her actions.
His anger had petered out in a yawn and he could not catch
up the thread of it.

"O.K. It's over. Let's forget it," he now suggested.

"It's over in one sense," she agreed.

"Oh, don't. You'll get the horrors. You know you will.
Now we can forgive one another?"

She felt as if ice-floes had congealed the stream of affec-

tion between them, but since he regarded it as a little scene, merely, a tiff, one of a series, a lovers' quarrel, she could only do her best to imagine that no lasting harm was done, nothing said irrevocably, nor thought so bitterly that they might not wake up to the same day in the same bed, eat breakfast together and meet and part from day to day, with seeming peace and equanimity.

CHAPTER 22

"ELEANOR, I HAVE had to hang about and waylay you." Roddy suddenly slid out of the shadows in the gateway of Saint Winifred's. "I have been mooning about round here for twenty minutes," he said peevishly. "They will think I have some evil design against this school."

Eleanor had not spoken a word. "This way," he said, gently encouraging her back in the way she had come. "I am in the most hopeless predicament and you are the only one who can help me."

"But it's getting dark, Roddy, and cold. Why can't we go indoors?"

"Out of the question. We will walk briskly and keep ourselves warm."

"But walk where to? I can't believe you are in any predicament so bad that we must catch our deaths of cold discussing it."

"I am. I am. I will talk as quickly as I can and you must listen to me."

She resigned herself, though tired, to walking back the way she had come, and thrust her hands up her wide sleeves for warmth. "Well then!"

"Eleanor! I hardly know how to tell you, but I have promised to be quick and that means I must be blunt. I have become involved in a little accident and the appalling thing is that I was in the company of another woman. Not Julia, I mean," he added. He would have liked some answer to this, but, getting none, continued: "It was like this . . . I had to go out in the brake . . . a little journey outside the town . . . I sometimes do have to . . . and it was so nice after tea, the weather I mean . . . and I said to this girl why not come along . . . it seemed the obvious thing . . ." Again he paused, but was forced to go on, quite uncertain of his cousin's reaction to it all.

"So she came. Shall we go up this road a little way? The trouble was we decided to get a drink and went a little off our route. Then we left the car and strolled down to the river, where a quite ghastly coincidence occurred. There was no one in sight, except a man waving frantically at us. Then to my amazement he suddenly jumped off the bank, into the river and began to do a hopeless sort of dog's paddle and then—oh, *awful, awful* . . ." He was walking quicker and quicker. ". . . a head appeared in the river and I realised that he'd gone in after someone. My good instincts got the better of me and I dived in. Well, somehow I got both back safely —they weren't far out. Put the little girl on her stomach and pressed the water out of her. She seemed all right after a while. Coming back in the car she suddenly revived and said 'thank you for saving me.' I asked her where she lived. "Don't you *know*?" she said. "Don't you *know* who I am? I'm . . ." He passed a hand wearily over his face . . . "I'm Felicity Mallory." He sighed.

"You'll be a Squadron Leader in the morning," said Eleanor.

"But, you see, there's too much to explain. The car—why I was there, why Mu . . . why I was not alone. You see?"

" Who are you frightened of—Julia or the Wing Co? " asked Eleanor brutally, for veils had been torn rather swiftly from her eyes.

" Both," he said simply.

" Well, what can we do or say? "

" That the woman was you. Felicity doesn't know you well, and, anyway, she was suffering from shock; but she would remember there *was* a woman. So would the man. He was a Town Councillor. It will be in the local papers."

" What were they doing there? "

" He was fishing. He saw the wretched girl wade out from some rushes with a net in her hand, fall into some weeds and disappear. The bank suddenly shelved, I suppose."

She considered. " All right. I was the woman. It *is* Julia you are frightened of, then, in the long run."

" Please don't! "

" What about the car? "

" I can't explain that. Anyhow, it turned out to be the Wing Co's good fortune. She'd have drowned if I hadn't turned off the road. As long as he never finds out about Mu . . . my friend."

" Let me get it all straight before we go home. I met you in the town as you were driving off, and you said: ' Why not come? ' It was the obvious thing to do," she added with complete malice. She had had an unsatisfactory evening in the draught at Mozart Terrace, listening to some of Mr Aldridge's adolescent poems in which symbols of revolution and of sex were mingled inevitably together—guns, blood and barricades, and the less generally referred-to parts of the body. A confidence like this she could have luxuriated in, sitting before a fire; but now, the intimacy, the delightful situation of Roddy pleading for her help, the idea of Julia vanquished, were all thrown away because she was made to pace the streets, up and down the pitch-dark unromantic

191

pavements, with her teeth chattering and the bones of her face aching with the cold.

"All the same, it doesn't convince me, Roddy. I'm a poor liar," she lied, knowing she was a magnificent one. "She'll catch me out easily."

"She absolutely mustn't!" he cried.

"Need we go farther? I think we are in someone's private drive."

"Oh, hell, I believe it's the back entrance of that confounded girls' school." He looked over the top of some close boarding and could make out the dark shapes of a row of poplars.

"We shall have a lot of wretched virgins after us."

Eleanor made no reply.

He took her arm and they turned back through the darkness.

"Why *did* you, Roddy?" she felt justified in asking. "I should have thought any other man. Not you."

"Oh, all men are swine," he boasted. "Not that there is anything in it."

"Are you sure?"

"Good God, yes. I've gone down in your estimation, I see, Eleanor."

"Yes. But that is *my* fault. I hero-worshipped you as a child. I made something of you you could never be."

"And what am I now?"

"Oh, nothing so very dreadful."

"I hope we manage all right." They turned the corner of the Crescent.

Julia was darning. They could not be sure how their story was being received, for she made no comment, sitting there with a black sock over her fist and her head bent.

"Thank God Oliver wasn't with her," she said at last. "She is quite sure to drown in the end." She bit off the wool

and folded the sock. " You will get promotion in the morn-
ing, Roddy," she said. " You will have a squadron of your
own at last. What a bit of luck it wasn't some junior officer's
child ! "

" Promotion doesn't depend on those things," he said,
smiling in his relief.

" Well, then, it ought," she said. " Whose clothes are
those ? "

" They are more or less Edwards'."

Julia got up to bring in the supper and Eleanor, having
escaped the witness-box, slipped upstairs to read the *Daily
Worker* and wash her hands. Curiously, it was Julia she
despised, not Roddy.

CHAPTER 23

FOR A COUPLE of days days Roddy experienced the
unpopularity of the lately bereaved. Having soberly
applauded his presence of mind his friends found nothing
more to say. Their tact and silence barred his way to the
old enjoyments. It was as if the others no longer expected
him to take part in their trivial pursuits. They bought him
a drink and left him in a corner. He found himself turning
the glossy pages of the *Tatler* and gazing at rich young
mothers with children wearing dungarees and pushing wheel-
barrows. Wartime society. The Wing Commander having,
with his wife, once thanked him, now appeared to be avoid-
ing him. He felt the injustice of the situation most keenly.

' It will all pass over,' he comforted himself. ' People forget
so quickly.'

This seemed to be so, for Edwards began, after a while, to jolly him. He was invited to join in at snooker. Life was returning.

"Wing Commander Mallory, sir," said the Corporal, handing him the telephone.

"Drink up," said Edwards, as Roddy came back. "What's his offer? Rings to the elbow and some marmalade on your hat? Least he can do."

"If he could do that much, why the hell doesn't he do it for himself? How many bloody years has he been a Wing-Co?"

"Ever since he stopped working at the hairdresser's. Another beer?"

"No, I have to go upstairs. The old man wants me."

"Perhaps he'll write you out a cheque."

"Or give you a marrow from the garden," someone else suggested.

"Oh God, that kid. If only it had been some other person's child."

"Quick, the line-book! What was it now? 'If only it had been some other person's child!' That's rich."

"Don't be such a bloody fool. I'm off."

"Trust Rod," said Edwards, when he had gone. "Just trust Rod. If he's got to jump into the cold water he'll be sure to fish out something worth while. 'If it had only been some other person's child!' Yes, that's lovely."

.

"Davenant."

"Sir."

"Oh, a signal has come through which will please you, I think."

"Thank you, sir."

"A Posting nearer home."

"Nearer home, sir?"

"The big city itself."

"I see, sir."

"I think your wife will be glad to get home."

Roddy was dumbfounded.

"Won't she?"

"We had hoped to settle here—rather an upheaval—I more or less told her I was fixed . . ."

"We never know that in the Service."

Roddy felt that this was more than unjust.

"Schools and so on . . . it's a pity chopping and changing . . ."

"Oliver has scarcely chopped or changed."

The Wing Commander began to fill his fountain-pen very slowly, smiling as he did so.

"And bombs . . ." Roddy went on desperately.

"Neither does the Service hold itself responsible for the evacuation of women and children."

"I see, sir." He stiffened himself, his face was redder than usual. He was furiously angry and wanted to strike the other man. There was very much he would have liked to say, many reminders, many recriminations. He moistened his lips. "*When* do I go, sir?"

"The posting's for the eighteenth. Two day's time. I can probably get you a couple of days extension on compassionate grounds, if it will be more convenient."

"Thank you, sir."

"There will be more hope of promotion for you there. Rather a dead end here. No wastage."

"No, sir."

"Good. Well, I'm glad you're pleased. Very kind regards to Mrs Davenant. Oh, and while I think of it, my wife asked me to hand this to you. A handkerchief your cousin lent

195

my little girl in the car after the accident. Very kind of her. My wife has washed it."

"Thank you, sir."

"Not at all."

For a moment they contemplated one another without words. "There is nothing you want to say?" asked the Wing Commander, when he had screwed on the top of his fountain-pen and wiped the nib carefully on a piece of blotting-paper.

"Nothing, sir."

"When I urged that your wife should come to live here, I did so in the hope that it might save your marriage."

"Thank you, sir." Roddy shook with anger and contempt.

"I have seen many homes broken by the war. You are a good officer—any report I have ever given will bear that out—I hoped for something better for you. I didn't know the sort of man you were—that you would use your wife to preserve the *status quo*, so that you might conduct your amours with a new safety and immunity because of her presence, that you would use her, in fact, to save yourself from your mistress."

The telephone buzzed and he put his hand towards it. "That will be all, Davenant." He lifted the receiver.

Roddy closed the door and found himself tiptoeing along the corridor. He went down the back stairs through the Waaf quarters because he could not face the others in the Ante-room. He let himself out of the backdoor and stood in a cobbled yard. It was a grey, sultry day and not a leaf stirred. He wiped his forehead and the palms of his hands with the little handkerchief he was clutching. 'Mistress!' he thought. 'Good Christ!' It was like the swine of a man to use such a word for what he and Edwards would have called a bit of a frippet. Also, he thought, it implied a financial arrangement which did not, in more than the

196

vaguest sense, exist. He folded the handkerchief again and was about to put it in his pocket when he caught sight of the name 'Muriel Parsons' printed on the hem.

.

"A Communist shouldn't be afraid of wasps," said Mr Speed, smacking one smartly to the ground with his hand. It was a very late, tired wasp, an easy prey.

"School to-morrow!" Eleanor sighed.

"You and Chris amaze me," said Sarge, perching himself on a pile of biscuit tins. "Two months' holiday and grumbles at the end of it."

"Schools would be all right, if it weren't for the children."

They fell silent as a customer came in and was served and went out.

"As a matter of fact and it's none of my business," began Mr Speed, drawing a wire through a piece of over-ripe cheese, "but I saw that Mr Aldridge in Murray's buying a second-hand Trotsky's *History of the Russian Revolution*."

Sarge clicked his tongue.

"You are like a couple of old ladies behind lace curtains," said Vera, coming downstairs on her way to a meeting.

"Where are you going, Vera?"

"Women's Guild."

"Have fun!"

She gave him a scornful look and went out.

"She's a feminist, really. Funny how feminists don't like being with other women. That dislike is at the bottom of it all. Turns them upside down. But all the same," said Sarge, balancing himself carefully, "I'm bound to say I'd be the same if I was one. A woman, I mean. So Chris is being a bad boy. Eleanor, you should take more care of him and not let him deviate like this."

"I'm not making any mischief," said Mr Speed. "No harm in buying a book. Or reading one for that matter. We are not fascists."

"You ought to have gone with Vera," Sarge told Eleanor. "It would ease her mind a lot if she had someone to help her when the baby's born—with the meetings, I mean."

"First I've heard of any baby," said Mr Speed.

"We don't tell the landlord in case he turns us out."

"First I've heard, too," said Eleanor boldly.

"First anyone has heard," said Sarge. He became excited suddenly and jumped off the biscuit tins. "Here come Leo and Kirsty!" He went to open the door to them. "Vera's going to have a baby," he said, as soon as they came in. . . .

"Oh, Lord, is that all?" Kirsty said in a tired voice. "I knew that ages ago." She glanced round at them all and went upstairs. When Eleanor looked again at Sarge, she saw that his excitement had vanished, and he had fallen into one of his old habits of biting contemplatively at a knuckle.

"I must go," she said. "I promised to be back for supper. They want to go out."

.

Julia took the news well; Oliver less well, and Eleanor with complete loss of self-control. From wrath and recrimination, she dropped to the pathos of the single woman bravely facing old age, supporting herself by her own industry, in which pursuit she was hindered and obstructed by the Royal Air Force and the Wing Commander, whom she had never liked and had never been able to understand.

Oliver was sent to bed, supper was brought in, and still she denunciated and explained her position.

"He imagines he's doing it for my benefit," said Roddy

198

at last. Supper was now over—he had eaten and was exhausted.

"It should be easy to disillusion him," Eleanor said.. "I shall have to stay on for another term. Apart from being obliged to give notice, I owe it to Threlly. I shall have to get lodgings." ('Mozart Terrace?' she wondered. 'Or live with Threlly and Cowper? The Vasco Road? Vera and the baby.' She saw herself as a part of that ménage— reliable, useful, unobtrusive at first; later, accepted, her worth assessed; and, finally, indispensable. 'How on earth did we manage before Eleanor came?' She was vague as to who should utter these words, for they would sound unnatural coming from anyone there, but uttered she was sure they would be).

Julia cut off a shaving of cheese and nibbled it.

"I notice you say nothing," Eleanor said sharply.

"It makes very little difference to me. I am a parasite. I follow my man round like a piece of luggage or part of a travelling harem. He is under contract to provide for me, but where he does so is for him to decide."

"It is not for me to decide," said Roddy loudly, annoyed by her speech. Obscurely he felt that it was a husband's business to make jokes (for such he took her remarks to be) about married life.

"War only sharpens contrasts, makes one see one's position more clearly. Hence—revolutions at the end of them."

"Are you intending to revolt, may I ask?"

"You shouldn't ask. It is never done. But I am not."

"What are we discussing?" cried Eleanor. "What *are* we discussing?" She got up and with one splendid movement gathered the dirty plates together. "You'll have to be off, if you're going to the Mess."

"I don't want to go," said Julia quickly.

"Nor I," said Roddy.

PICKERING PUBLIC LIBRARY
CENTRAL BRANCH

"For once you are agreeing about something," said Eleanor. "Sweet are the uses of adversity."

CHAPTER 24

FOR THE NEXT few days Roddy expected—and received—the most unappetising of meals, odds and ends to be finished up and Julia's mind not on her cooking. Terrible concoctions were brought to the table—bits of tinned salmon mashed with potatoes, vegetables scarcely warmed through in a white sauce; sometimes, for a sweet, five or six different dishes to choose from with a little piece in each, a couple of prunes, some stewed pears, a wedge of chocolate blancmange hard at the edges, and some yellowing milk pudding.

Eleanor was beginning to pack, sorting out what she would take back to London with her and what she would leave at Sunnybank to await her return at the end of the holidays. Her manner was now cool and flippant, especially towards Roddy, who grew uneasy. They eyed one another in alternate glances across the table at meals.

"What will you have, Eleanor?" Julia asked. It was the last lunch but one in Mrs Lippincote's house, and the air of make-shift, of being ready to fly away at any moment, pervaded the room.

"Well, I'd really prefer the pears, unless Roddy . . . and I'll finish up the blancmange for you."

There was a prune each and a solid spoonful of cold rice for the others. They ate it without appreciation—dully and without a word. Once Roddy would have complained, but to-day, for some reason or other, he did not.

When Eleanor and Oliver had left them alone, Roddy came behind Julia's chair and kissed her.

"You have taken this very well."

"Thank you, Roddy."

"Very well indeed. Something so unforeseen, making so much work for you."

"Many other women have to do as much and more."

"I know, my dear, but that is not your usual kind of reasoning. I have sometimes tried to put forward that point of view over other matters, and I have been met with a storm of abuse or sarcasm."

"What other matters?"

"Well—Oliver being ill and other things."

"What other things?"

"I can't for the life of me remember," he said, and laughed and kissed her again.

"Anyhow, Oliver being ill is much worse than this."

Her long, heavy hair could not be constrained. As Roddy bent to kiss her, one frond after another slithered down and hairpins fell into her lap. She cursed and thrust them in wildly. He tried to help her and rolled up bunches of hair in quite a clever way.

"You used to brush my hair every night when we were first married," she said, staring before her at the wreckage on the table.

"Yes, you would sit on the floor between my knees and I would brush it out long and smooth. It always looked bright and full of colour—streaks of red and gold and brown—with the light shining down on it. It is something I must remember to do. I've forgotten how to be a good husband."

"There is never time nowadays. These awful hairpins. They were the only kind Corporal Crook could get."

"What do you mean?"

He took his hands off her hair and put them in his pockets.

"When he came with the marrows, he asked if there was any shopping he could do. I said not to bother, but if he should see any hairpins . . ."

"My God, he's supposed to be in the R.A.F."

"He asked."

"It isn't for him to ask. *I* tell him what to do with his time. He doesn't decide for himself and he's not your servant."

"No. I wish he were."

"And hairpins! Oh, Julia, the Squadron will be full of this."

"And such heavy black things, too!" she sighed. "No good at all. I'm sorry, Roddy. I didn't understand."

"No, I'm afraid you didn't. Well, I must go. When will you grow up, Julia?"

"If I am not grown up now, I see little hope of it."

She pushed back her chair and stood up.

'Oh, I'm glad I'm going,' she thought. 'I'm very, very glad I'm going.'

Mrs Lippincote would soon be back in her own home; perhaps she had been waiting for them to go, praying for them to go, for Miss Phyllis could not settle at the Saint Winifred's Hotel, which was Mrs Whapshott's explanation.

Already, boxes and packing cases stood about the house, half-filled, or with piles of folded clothes beside them. Oliver had put his books into a carton, with a lump of multi-coloured plasticine, some snail-shells, a parachute Felicity had made from a handkerchief, a piece of flint which was probably an arrow-head and some blood-alleys.

Julia was determined to get one case packed and corded up that afternoon. 'I don't care how lonely I am,' she thought as she went upstairs, 'I don't care whether Eleanor is with me or not, or if the sky rains bombs, I shall never

move again.' So she felt, as she packed, that she was definitely sending the things home for the last time.

She opened a drawer and took out an assortment of shapeless, washed-out woollies, which she would never wear again, but felt she might. Among these were some cakes of soap in cellophane, the occasion for such luxury never having arrived. Then a bundle of photographs, mounted on cardboard—mostly groups of football or cricket teams, with Roddy sitting always somewhere near the centre or holding a silver cup or shield. Julia, in her picture, was only one of four hundred other girls in white linen tunics and stood near the end of the strip rather blurred and unfocussed. She looked merely cheerful and healthy, as far as one could see anything of her. And so did Roddy in his football group. His lip curled more in those days, his hair hung in a fringe above his eyes, his rather square-shaped knees were as if sculped; but the hands (which were spread round a football on which was whitewashed 'Ist XI 1926') were the same, and she recognised with a little shock the wide fingers, the shape of the nails, the man's hands before the man. "Oh, Roddy!" she cried aloud, but softly, kneeling before the drawer, mourning Roddy's boyhood for him.

Why keep all this? she wondered, remembering Mrs Lippincote's bureau downstairs, that nightmare of hoarding, and taking up a small packet of letters from a man she had once thought of marrying, but who had not thought of marrying her. *My own Julia, how nice to have you for a dear friend*, she now glimpsed, written on white crackly paper in very black ink. She knew it all by heart, knew how it continued—*It makes me think much nicer things may be coming to me in the future*. Whether they did or not she had no idea, certainly they had not come via her. 'But why any longer desire the remembrance of having been cherished—however meagrely—by other men than Roddy?

I never wanted to be a Madame Bovary. That way for ever —literature teaches us as much, if life doesn't—lies disillusion and destruction. I would rather be a good mother, a fairly good wife, and at peace.'

She gathered up all the old photographs and letters and went downstairs. Sitting on the rug by the drawing-room fire, with a waste-paper basket beside her, she began to tear up letters until her wrists ached.

In a little while, Eleanor brought the Wing Commander there. She looked at the strange scene for a moment and then went upstairs again.

" I came to say goodbye to you."

" I hoped you would."

" I am very sorry about it all."

" Everyone seems sorry for me, but really London is my home, you know."

" Yes, I suppose you have many friends there."

" My friends are a bit scattered since the war. Otherwise I don't think I could have come here." She paused for a moment and rammed down the torn letters in the basket. " I am clearing up, you see. I am about to start life afresh."

" Why do you say that? "

" Well, I have finished with one thing and am beginning another. I am rather one of those people who can only start being good at the New Year or on some other special occasion. I want to try to be more grown-up and less like myself all the time, try to be more sympathetic to Roddy, more patient with Oliver, and more benevolent "—she glanced at the door and grimaced—" towards Eleanor."

He had fanned out a handful of photographs as if he were playing Happy Families. " I have one of you as a little girl. Very fat," he said. He held up the picture of a child kneeling on a bearskin rug and aiming a small bow and arrow carefully away from the photographer.

"Cupid," she murmured, taking the cards from him and sorting them out, throwing some into the basket, keeping others in her lap.

"May I read one of your school reports?"

"Oh, yes, I should like to hear it myself."

"In the summer term of 1926 your interest in Algebra was volatile and unstable. Games: Too talkative."

"They try to impress the customers. Here is Roddy in his first long trousers."

But he was not interested in Roddy's long trousers.

"And here is Oliver, looking like Before Taking Virol. However did we keep him going." She put that photograph on one side, with Roddy's. She looked up at him for a moment and then swept all the clutter aside.

"Shall we meet again?"

"We might."

"After the war?"

"Why wait until then?"

"I have never found out much about you," she regretted and, though she waited, he only said: "I am sometimes in London. Perhaps you would lunch with me?"

"I should like to," she said, without enthusiasm, for she knew, at her age, that people mean different things in different places.

"Corporal Crook is reporting here in the morning with some eggs for your journey."

She smiled. 'Egg sandwiches,' she thought, 'we are back where we started.'

"Is there anything else?"

"You have thought of everything yourself. In fact, you have always been thoughtful and sympathetic towards me."

"No. There is some acid in me which curdles the very milk of human kindness."

He stood up and leaned against the mantelpiece. She

stood up, too, and was reaching for the cigarette box when he took her hand and held it.

"Then if there is nothing more, goodbye."

Her eyes brimmed readily, as she could not prevent them doing on such an occasion.

"Don't come out. I can find my way. There is a little package for you on the table in the hall. Goodbye, my dear."

She let him go and turned to the window to wave to him as he passed down the drive. In a minute he appeared and when he was almost out of sight he remembered, apparently, and turned and saluted.

She felt acutely depressed until, looking out over the boring front garden with its shrubs, the thought of London once again raised the level of her spirits.

As she moved away from the window, her thoughts were with Mr Taylor, his life as she knew it or guessed it, his beginnings and his end, the mother he had imagined and the mother he really had, his sister . . . 'and what of her?'

She picked up the paper-baskets and carried them out. In the hall she remembered the Wing Commander once more and took up the parcel which lay on the table. It was a copy of *Wuthering Heights*, with her name written in it, beneath his own which was scored through. Inside was a card with a piece of dried heather pinned to it and inscribed : "Picked near Wuthering Heights on August 18, 1920." The purple flower-bells had nearly all fallen away. 'He is an incurable sentimentalist,' she thought, closing the book.

"What have you been doing?" Eleanor asked coming downstairs in her outdoor clothes.

"Tearing up all my letters from Roddy," Julia said, and lifting the two baskets once more, went out to the kitchen.

Eleanor, looking a little alarmed, gave a quick glance at the dried heather and then let herself out of the front door and hastened away in the direction of Vasco Street.

CHAPTER 25

OLIVER AND FELICITY wandered along the main road, with nothing to do but to kill time. They were already lost to one another; the few hours that were left could hold no enjoyment for them and they wanted, each separately and deeply, to be rid of the other.

"There's no use going to the river," said Felicity, "if we can't go again to-morrow." An isolated pleasure seemed threatening and empty, useless unless there was the hope of more of the same kind coming their way in the future.

"Too windy, anyhow," said Oliver, lifting his shoulders to his ears.

They abhorred the idea of making an occasion of this last day, of one of those 'last times', which adults cannot, in their sentimentality, resist. They knew their friendship was done for and that they were quite helpless.

They paused to look in through the gates of 'Sunnybank'. 'I've missed that,' thought Oliver. 'But I expect they'll have some other awful thing ready for me.'

Large leaves like pieces of brown paper cluttered the mossy drive. A grey squirrel rippled down the branches of a tree. Felicity threw a stone at it. "They're only rats," she said. She had thrown very hard, with a little jet of anger, and now her cheeks were red. A woman came to a window and rapped on the pane with a very white hand. Then she put the hand up to her dark hair and moved away.

"It's that Cowper woman," said Oliver.

They crossed the main road and turned into the Crescent. A man in an apron cleaned the brass plate outside the school; mops came out of windows; a piano-tuner stumbled over an arpeggio, smells of disinfectant and floor polish floated

out to them and all the white furniture at the bedroom windows seemed ready and expectant. Felicity walked by without looking.

At the gate of Mrs Lippincote's they met Corporal Crook carrying an empty basket. Felicity gave him a searching look. "I thought it was funny you weren't out with your Flight. We met them just now doing about a hundred to the minute."

"Not my funeral, ma'am," he said cheerfully.

"It looked as if it was somebody's," said Oliver, with a sudden uncontrolled guffaw. Felicity shrieked with laughter.

The Corporal held out his hand to Oliver. "Well, I shall miss you with your smart answers. Nice knowing you. Happy landings, son. As for her . . ." he nodded his head. "She thinks she's the Daughter of the Regiment." It was his turn to laugh and he went off down the Crescent doing so.

They wandered listlessly into the garden. Time seemed paid out slowly, bit by bit, like a rope. Oliver picked two spotted-laurel leaves and with a pin wrote ' Felicity ' on one and his own name on the other. "It's a child's game. Keep it next to your skin and if the writing turns brown it means we always—like one another. It's only silly, because, of course, it always does turn brown." She took hers and slipped it down the neck of her jersey. Oliver suddenly wanted to throw his away but he was a kind little boy and rather self-consciously opened the front of his shirt and dropped it in.

"Oliver!" called Julia from the front door. "Felicity! Your mother telephoned for you, Felicity."

"What does she want?"

"She wants you, my dear. I didn't ask what for. You had better run along at once. Where are you going, Oliver?"

He turned with surprise. "Upstairs."

"Well, you won't see Felicity any more. Aren't you going to say goodbye?"

"Goodbye."

They looked at one another with boredom.

"Goodbye, Felicity," said Julia, stooping and kissing her cheek. "I hope we may meet again one day."

She ducked her head and was off down the drive, trotting like a pony, tossing her fringe out of her eyes.

Oliver went upstairs to his bedroom. He stood by his box, fingering the label, and thinking of his mother, at whose mercy he seemed, who considered, apparently, one friend as good as another for a child. 'Oh dear it is a half and half day,' he sighed. He lifted the cover of Mrs Lippincote's *Wide, Wide World* and took a last look at the little girl in white stockings, then he went to the window and looked out across the empty playing fields of Saint Winifred's School for Young Ladies.

.

Felicity curled up under her eiderdown, sobbing. 'If it were a year,' she thought, 'or ten years or even fifteen years. If we were grown up and could make plans. Fifteen years would pass and be over one day. But "never" is with you always.'

The laurel-leaf pricked her flat chest, and she took it from under her liberty bodice and looked at it. It was warm from her body and 'Oliver' was engraved on it in brown. Although he had said this invariably happened, she was a little comforted and lay, with the leaf against her cheek, in the peace that follows violent emotion.

. . . .

"You have forgotten this," said Eleanor, picking up the white china swan from the mantelpiece.

"I haven't. I never really wanted it," said Julia.

" What's in this box ? "

" Oh, the Christmas-tree decorations. We needn't have brought them, but we didn't know that. I think I can hear Roddy."

" What's for supper ? "

" I left out a tin of sardines."

" Then what are the eggs boiling for ? "

" Oh, they're for sandwiches for the train. I'll chop them up this time to make a change."

"That won't make much of a change," said Roddy, throwing down his hat and smoothing his forehead.

" What else is there ? The cheese has all gone and somehow or other we don't seem to have any caviare in the house."

All their tempers were frayed.

" Mrs Whapshott gone ? "

" I don't think so."

" She'll have a fine old mess to clear up to-morrow," said Roddy.

" It's what she's paid for," said Julia, for she would be out of the house soon and could afford to adopt this grand attitude. " Did you leave the front door open, Roddy ? "

" No."

" There's an awful draught swirling round my ankles. I think you must have done."

Phyllis Lippincote walked in, her face quite brilliant, her arms full of photographs in silver frames. " To-morrow, we are coming back. These . . ." she bunched up the frames to her with a gesture of love . . . " These turn it back once more into our home. They never seemed right at Saint Winifred's." With great zest she began to distribute them round the room—pictures of the boys in Eton collars, with silky fringes on their brows; Mr Lippincote with the mild and waxen countenance murderers usually have; Mrs hold-

ing paper roses, as the Greek philosophers hold rolls of parchment—authoritatively.

"Enough of that, Miss Phyllis!" said Mrs Whapshott sharply. She was standing in the doorway with her coat on and her rolled-up apron in the basket. "You come along back to Madam."

Phyllis had completed her work and now stood back to survey the room. "We must make it pleasant for the wedding," she said. "And now I must go back to fetch some more."

"Bolt the door!" cried Roddy, as soon as Mrs Whapshott had led her away. "Shoot the bolt along and stand well back from the windows."

"You really are cut out to do noble things," said Julia aloofly. "How you can handle a situation."

"How can you talk to Roddy like that?" asked Eleanor.

"By not thinking him as wonderful as you do."

"How dare you!"

"Girls," said Roddy, foolishly. "For heaven's sake! We're all tired. Let's not make it worse than it is. Let's have the sardines and I'll get some tea." That they were quarrelling over him did not please him as once it would have done; for he was apprehensive these last few days and wanting to be out of the place as quickly as possible.

"I don't think Roddy at all marvellous," said Eleanor with a level and penetrating look at him.

That did not please Julia either. "I suppose he now compares unfavourably with your little carpentry master."

"Julia! And I will not be discussed in this way."

"There's no love in this house," cried Eleanor. "There never has been. You've despised me always and gone to very little trouble to disguise your . . ."

"Despision," said Julia gently. She was in a fiendish mood.

"You don't even love your child," Eleanor swept on. "You've ruined Roddy. He would have been a good husband to you, but you threw away his love and have lost him."

"Did I, Eleanor? Roddy, have I? Have I lost your love?"

"Eleanor! Behave yourself. You are making a scene. Then when you have had all the pleasure of making it you will want the added pleasure of apologising. And we shall not indulge you. I warn you. We shall accept no apologies."

"There will be no need to apologise. I shan't need to gloss things over so that we may endure living together, for I am not going to live with you any more."

"Then when are you going?" Julia asked.

"Since it will be embarrassing for us to meet again—I shall go now."

"Oh, please, let's not be like this," Roddy begged them.

"And so I have lost your love," said Julia, turning on him. "Without noticing it, since I have not Eleanor's perception—or inside information."

Roddy looked uneasy, she was forced to notice. It was not merely the recoil of a man from a women's quarrel.

"How *did* you notice, Eleanor?"

"You are mocking me, I know. I have at least learnt to recognise when you do that. You have mocked at everything I care for—crumbled my enthusiasm time and time again—and turned away, leaving me nothing. Now, *you* have nothing."

"Oh, this is frightful," Roddy shouted.

"I knew you hated me, but not as much as this," Julia said calmly. "So, Roddy, you have been faithless?"

Eleanor's ugly red deepened. "I didn't . . ." she began.

Julia turned to her gravely. "But you did," she said. "You did mean me to know that. How did you find out?"

Eleanor mumbled.

Turning to Roddy, Julia asked: "Do you want this other woman . . . or women . . . or do you want me?"

In fury, Roddy said: "It was not women—it was hardly even one woman. Eleanor, you are to pack and go."

"I didn't wish . . ."

"Yes, for a long time, you have been wishing," Julia cried. "I see it now. You could have spoken earlier and relieved yourself. It has been a 'worm i' the bud' to you." Instinctively she looked at Mrs Lippincote's wedding group. "We might have had this little scene a long time ago. We should all have been the better for it—if one can ever be the better for a scene, and I incline towards Roddy's opinion about that. Well, Eleanor would have been the better for it. To me, it has always been a matter of indifference."

"Always?"

"Yes, all the time, Roddy."

"I see." He was trembling. "How did you . . .?"

"Oh, in the traditional way," she said lightly. "Going through one's husband's pockets. How wives do discover things."

She saw again the bedroom as she had seen it on their first evening in the house, tired from her journey, the pink lights in the mahogany and the green-filled windows. Now, tired again, she sank down in her chair, lifted first one foot then the other from her shoes and smiled.

"For months," she said, "I have skated on thin ice. I shall be glad not to do it again." She regarded her ankles, as if she took her words literally.

Since they had not addressed her for some time, nor asked her advice, Eleanor rose and left the room. They heard her running upstairs as if in terror.

"Here we are then!" said Julia. "Husband and wife, alone together. On either side of—not our hearth but a

borrowed one. I didn't read it, really," she confessed. "Not any of your letters. I said that only to take the sweetness from her *dénouement*."

She knew, though, she had held such a letter in her hand that first evening. 'And if I didn't read it because I didn't care,' she thought, 'I am absolutely done for.'

"Nothing has happened," she said, for he was knocked off his balance, as only a man of action can be. "We are still the same people. Why look like that?"

But Roddy wanted love only where there was homage as well, and admiration. He did not want merely to be reckoned at his own worth.

"How can you love what you do not respect?" he asked bitterly.

"Women have to," she replied, feeling he was playing into her hand, like a character on the stage, grateful to him for giving her this chance, as if he had given her a cue in a play. "I have never admired you, Roddy, in the ways in which you expected admiration. In which women are supposed to admire men."

There were sounds from above of Eleanor opening and shutting drawers and dropping boxes—or so it seemed—all over the floor.

"I wonder where she'll go," said Julia.

"It isn't Eleanor, it's us!" cried Roddy. "Who cares what happens to her?"

"I don't care much," said Julia. "I am only inquisitive."

On her way to the window to draw the curtains, she laid her hands on his shoulders and smiled.

"If we could see one another as real people . . ." she began.

"You are inquisitive about little things, but about this . . ."

"I am a coward," she agreed.

Then she went across the room and took a curtain in each

214

hand and was about to draw them across the window when she laughed. "Ah, look!" she cried. "There goes Mr Aldridge down the road. He should have been dead months ago."

And with a great rattle and flourish she drew Mrs Lippincote's damask curtains across the window for the last time.

THE END

VIRAGO MODERN CLASSICS

The first Virago Modern Classic, *Frost in May* by Antonia White, was published in 1978. It launched a list dedicated to the celebration of women writers and to the rediscovery and reprinting of their works. Its aim was, and is, to demonstrate the existence of a female tradition in fiction which is both enriching and enjoyable. The Leavisite notion of the 'Great Tradition', and the narrow, academic definition of a 'classic', has meant the neglect of a large number of interesting secondary works of fiction. In calling the series 'Modern Classics' we do not necessarily mean 'great' — although this is often the case. Published with new critical and biographical introductions, books are chosen for many reasons: sometimes for their importance in literary history; sometimes because they illuminate particular aspects of womens' lives, both personal and public. They may be classics of comedy or storytelling; their interest can be historical, feminist, political or literary.

Initially the Virago Modern Classics concentrated on English novels and short stories published in the early decades of this century. As the series has grown it has broadened to include works of fiction from different centuries, different countries, cultures and literary traditions. In 1984 the Victorian Classics were launched; there are separate lists of Irish, Scottish, European, American, Australian and other English-speaking countries; there are books written by Black women, by Catholic and Jewish women, and a few relevant novels by men. There is, too, a companion series of Non-Fiction Classics constituting biography, autobiography, travel, journalism, essays, poetry, letters and diaries.

By the end of 1988 over 300 titles will have been published in these two series, many of which have been suggested by our readers.

11862